LONG ROAD TO TOMORROW

The Complete Saga, Volume 2

Arthur Leo Zagat

LONG ROAD TO TOMORROW

The Complete Saga, Volume 2

ALTUS PRESS • 2014

EDITED AND DESIGNED BY

Matthew Moring

PUBLISHING HISTORY

"Sunrise Tomorrow" originally appeared in June 8 & 15, 1940 issue of *Argosy* magazine. Copyright 1940 by The Frank A. Munsey Company. Copyright renewed 1967 and assigned to Steeger Properties, LLC. All Rights Reserved.

"Long Road to Tomorrow" originally appeared in March 1, 8, 15 & 22, 1941 issue of *Argosy* magazine. Copyright 1941 by The Frank A. Munsey Company. Copyright renewed 1968 and assigned to Steeger Properties, LLC. All Rights Reserved.

THANKS TO

Joel Frieman, Don O'Malley, Rob Preston & Christopher Roden

CONTENTS

SUNRISE TOMORROW

CHAPTER 1

'WARE PLANE!

"WHY DON'T they come, Normanfenton?" Dikar asked the tall, loosely built man beside him. "What are the Asafrics waitin' for?" They were standing in front of a gray, grim building and it rose almost as high, it seemed, as the Mountain that, till two nights ago, had been all the world Dikar and the Bunch knew

"Why don't they come to punish us for what we have done?"

Two nights ago the Boys and Girls of the Bunch, with the Beast Folk from the tangled woods below the Mountain, had fought to take from the Asafrics this great gray building and the other gray buildings that made up West Point.

A pitiful few against the black- and yellow-faced many, with bows and arrows and knives against rifles and huge guns, they had fought and won. But the loom of these walls was now a gray weight overhanging Dikar, and a heavy dread of what brooded beyond the hills had taken the place of the blazing joy of that victory.

"Maybe they don't quite believe we have done it, son." Normanfenton's massive head, black-bearded, lined with worry and sadness, did not turn to Dikar "Or maybe they're waiting to find out how we did it, how strong we are and what weapons we have."

From under the dark, bushy brows thoughtful eyes watched the bustle on the grassy, flat field that stretched before them, ten times as big as the Clearing on the Mountain. "From what

1

the farmers who have been flocking in here have to say, not many of the black soldiers who escaped us can have gotten through to New York. All over the countryside they were waylaid that night, their throats cut, their bodies hidden."

"At least we have accomplished that much, sir," Walt put in from the other side of Normanfenton. "Our people would not have dared even to scowl at an Asafric, much less lay a finger on one, before we pulled this thing off. At least we have given them courage."

"Courage?" Normanfenton's gnarled hand, bigger even than Dikar's, closed slowly into a fist. "God grant that it does not turn out to be only rashness we have inspired in them, that we have not merely brought on them even worse cruelties than they already have had to bear.

"I am not at all sure, this morning, that this adventure of ours is anything but sheer madness. We are still without news

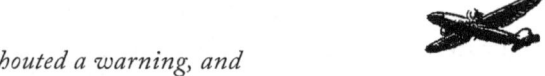

Dikar shouted a warning, and West Point was a tumult of cries and the thunder of guns.

from beyond the circle of cannon and machine-gun nests that give us a little safety here."

"We ought to hear something pretty soon." Walt came only to Normanfenton's shoulder. "I've just come from where Colonel Dawson and his men have been working to rebuild the radio."

When Dikar first brought him to the Mountain from the woods below it, Walt had looked and smelled more like an animal than a man, his rags crusted with dirt, his eyes, somehow both frightened and fierce, peering out of a mask of matted hair. "They hope to have it in shape very soon now, and then we'll be able to get in touch with the Secret Net." Now he had scraped the hair from his hollow cheeks and lean jaw, and in West Point had got new clothing to wear, gray-blue with shiny buttons. "But the waiting is hard, I'll grant you that."

"Yes," Normanfenton sighed. "The waiting is hard." He too was dressed in one of the gray-blue uniforms great piles of

which had filled a stone house at the other end of the big field that was called the Plain. "But I have a notion that it is a good omen—to be waiting here."

"A good omen, sir?"

"If history does repeat itself." The big, gnarled hand gestured to the scene before them. "Look at the men drilling out there. More than two hundred years ago other men marched and countermarched on that very Plain, their commander-in-chief a man named George Washington.

"Look at the women and children and old men crowded around watching, no longer sodden with despair, hope dawning in haggard faces that so long have known no hope. Just so must the Colonials have looked who watched Washington's men."

"I see what you mean, sir," Walt's face lit up. "The parallel is amazing. Look. The Continentals had their Indian allies and we have Dikar's Boys from the Mountain, strolling about half-naked, knives in their belts, mows in their hands and quivers slung over their shoulders."

WHEN THEY'D first found the store of gray-blue clothes, the Beast Folk, throwing away the rags that hung rotting from their starved bodies, had sung and danced with joy in their brave, new dress.

But not so the Boys and Girls of the Bunch. They had liked the shining buttons and the color of the uniforms, but the stuff had itched their skins and cramped their limbs, and they had torn it off again, refusing to have any more to do with it.

"Yes," Normanfenton agreed. "Do you recall, Walt, that Washington once wrote about this fort where we are starting our own rebellion? 'It is the key to America.'"

The Bunch had wanted to stay the way they'd always been on the Mountain; the Girls wearing only thigh-length reed skirts and circlets woven from leaves to cover their deepening breasts, the Boys only small aprons of twigs split and deftly plaited. Dikar could not yet quite understand why Norman-fenton had said no, but Normanfenton was the leader and he must be obeyed, and so they'd worked out what Walt called a compromise.

In the little stone house there far across the Plain that had been given the Bunch for their own the Girls took from their beds soft, white cloth and cut this into short lengths and wound the strips about themselves. When he saw one of these wrappings on Marilee, Dikar's gray-eyed mate, Normanfenton had called it a sarong, but Dikar knew only that Marilee was no less beautiful than before, and that she thrilled him as always.

He himself had led the Boys up on the wooded hill beyond which curved the farthermost line of pillboxes, and had brought down a fawn with a single arrow. Scraping the hide clean, he had draped it up over his right shoulder and about his trunk and thighs.

" 'The key to America,'" Walt repeated. "Yes, I recall reading that."

Dikar's broad brow furrowed. He had learned since they came here that a key was a little iron that would make a door open, but he couldn't figure out how West Point could be that.

Biggest of the three, broad-shouldered, his spread legs stalwart as two saplings, his lean belly plaited with flat muscle, he was a puzzled youth trying to understand the talk of two oldsters.

The fawn's fur lay golden-brown against the living bronze of his skin, sun-dusted with gold. His thick mop of hair and silken young beard were bright-golden, and the clear, deep blue of his eyes was gold-fringed by their long lashes.

"And you recall that those who held this key," Normanfenton was saying, "were as poorly equipped, as meagerly trained as we are, that they faced an enemy as powerful. But they won liberty for America."

"They won it, yes." Though there was sunlight upon it, a shadow darkened Walt's gaunt face. "But their descendants lost it. America had grown great, so great that we were certain none would dare to attack us. We forgot the warning that 'eternal vigilance is the price of freedom.' And so, when the black and yellow hordes swept up from under the round of the world, we were unprepared, and though we fought desperately we were beaten, and liberty was dead in the land."

"Not dead, my boy," Normanfenton said softly. "Only chained. If they who once gathered here were not dismayed by the appalling odds against them, why should we be? With faith in God and ourselves—" A cry broke in on him.

IT WAS a deep-toned howl that filled the air with fear, that rose and fell and rose again and broke the gray lines of marching men, broke the close-packed border of watchers into dark fragments scurrying toward the gray buildings like brown leaves driven by some sudden storm wind.

" 'Plane!" Dikar sent his deep-chested shout ringing across the field. " 'Ware plane!" Someone of the Bunch might not know, might have forgotten what the siren meant. " 'W-a-a-re plane."

The other two dived into the safety of the great building behind them but Dikar leaped out into the rushing crowd. He was threading deftly through it, was running lithely toward the long, low House, far across the wide and open field, that was the dwelling of the Bunch.

Beneath the siren's howling a little girl whimpered in fright. A little boy cried out, thinly, "Mom! Where are you, Mom?"

Dikar's throat went dry and he was cold all through, remembering, out of a Long-Ago vague as the memory of a dream, a little boy that was himself crying, 'Mom! Where are you, Mom?' as Dick Carr ran through a city's night-swallowed streets, cries of other little children all about him, over him a siren's howl, rising and falling and rising again and filling the dreadful night with the last alarm that city was ever to know.

All of a sudden the Plain was empty except for Dikar loping across its wide green. The wail of the siren was fading and Dikar heard now a new sound somewhere in the over-arching blue, a low hum such as the wild bee makes.

As he ran, Dikar looked up to find the thing that made the sound. He saw long black fingers lift above a jagged roof-edge to point slantingly southward, saw in the sunny south sky a tiny black speck that grew even in the instant he saw it. It grew and became a black hawk soaring on outstretched, motionless wings, became a black and threatening plane small-seeming enough to be held on his two spread hands.

And Dikar remembered, out of a long-ago Time of Fear, just such planes flying high over a doomed city, remembered the death that had dropped from their bellies, the thunder of death that had shaken the city beneath him. And Dikar was young, and he did not want to die.

CHAPTER 2

HUNTSMEN, WHAT QUARRY?

THUNDER BOOMED in the sky as Dikar ran. The thunder came from the guns on the rooftops. Little puffs of white cloud spotted the blue around the black plane, but it came on.

It was climbing upward on a long slant. More cloud-flowers blossomed in the sky. Soft and white, they trailed the black bird across the blue, but the plane was lifting itself above the reach of the guns.

Dikar felt the coolness of shadow about him and knew he had reached the little House toward which all this time he'd been running. He stopped, stood staring upward.

"Dikar!" a clear, sweet voice cried his name from inside the House. "Dikar, you big silly, stop standin' out there. You'll get hurt."

"No, I won't, Marilee." A white pole rose straight and proud out of the middle of the Plain and from its high top waved a bright flag, striped white and red, and star-spangled on deep blue. "The plane's too high up to hurt anybody."

Circling now in the sky above the flag, the plane looked no

bigger than when Dikar first saw it, so he knew it must be awful high. The guns, too, knew it was so high there was no use their trying to reach it and so they had stopped thundering. "It's just flyin' around and around, like the baldy eagle that has its nest on the dead pine at the Mountain's tip-top."

"The little birds hide when the baldy eagle's in the sky." Marilee's voice was very near. "But you haven't the sense of a sparrow."

Dikar turned and saw her coming out of the House's deep stone archway, her brown hair sweeping down over her shoulders, sweeping down about her warm, brown slimness to her sandaled, tiny feet. "Come inside, you big ninny." The sun made red glints in Marilee's hair, and anger made red glints in the gray of her eyes.

"Get inside yourself," Dikar exclaimed, his throat suddenly tight with fear for his mate. "Get back inside, you little fool!" He had hold of her and was half-pushing, half-carrying her into the dark inside the House. "You're a nut, comin' out—"

She twisted loose from him, was a slender shadow in the shadows. "I thought the plane was too high to hurt anybody," she panted, "or am I wrong thinkin' I heard you say it is?"

"I said it is." Dikar tried to grin, but his lips were still stiff. "An' I'm sure it is." He could see her better now. "But it might swoop down, an'— Gosh, Marilee! You're beautiful when you're mad." His arm slid around her warm, soft body, drawing her to him and all of a sudden she was trembling against him and there was a sob in her breast. "Oh, Dikar," Marilee sobbed. "When I saw you runnin' across the Plain, all alone… Why did you do that, Dikar? Why didn't you go right inside the Big House where you were, like all the others did when the siren started?"

"Because you weren't in the Big House, there across the Plain where I was. You were here, and if the danger came true, I wanted to be here with you, to protect you if I could or to die with you if I couldn't, because without you I do not want to live."

Very simply he said this. In that long-ago Time of Fear when the Old Ones hid the Bunch on the Mountain from the Asafrics they were little children—Dikar, the oldest of them, only eight.

Soon after, the Old Ones were buried under the fall of the slanting hill along whose top had run the only way to reach the Mountain without help. The Boys and Girls of the Bunch, growing up without any older person among them, had kept the simple ways, the simple speech, of their childhood. Its simple frankness. There had been no one to teach them to be ashamed of speaking out their thoughts, their deepest feelings.

"I wouldn't think life worth livin', Marilee, with you dead."

"I know that, Dikar." Marilee's head lifted from Dikar's chest and her eyes were brilliant. "But you have no right to risk losin' your life just for me. You don't belong to me any more, or even to the Bunch of which you were Boss so long. You belong to the Far Land now, to the land for which that flag stands."

She pointed out through the doorway into the brightness. "You are too important to America to risk losin' your life just on account of me."

THE BLACK plane was no longer circling the sky above the flag. It had flown over the hills to the west and even its hum was gone from the sky. Doors were opening all around the Plain, and people coming out.

"No, Marilee," Dikar answered, and his tone was low, troubled. "I am not important to America at all. Look. The guns kept that plane so high that it could do us no harm. Could our bonarrers have done that? Of course not. That is how little use I am now, in all that has to be done before America is freed."

"But Dikar, you were a fine Boss on the Mountain, a wise leader—"

"Wise enough as Boss of the few Boys and Girls I knew as I know myself, on the Mountain whose ways I know. But the people of this Far Land are strange to me, the ways of this land strange ways. The beginnin' of bein' wise is in knowin', and it's Normanfenton who knows the ways of the people, of the land. It is Normanfenton who must be wise for us now, Normanfenton who must lead us. Don't you see that, Marilee?"

"I can see that you can't be boss any more, but you can fight."

"With what? My hands? This knife in my belt? I am not needed any more."

"No." Marilee laid her little hand on his arm, her face very serious. "But I've got a feelin' there still is work only you can do, an'—Oh!" Her eyes widened, looking suddenly past Dikar to where there was a sudden shuffling footfall in the doorway. "There's a man."

One of his legs was stiff and dragged after him as he shuffled in. He stopped in front of them, blinking the outside brightness out of his eyes. Dikar made out on his forehead a healed burn in the form of a star, the mark the Asafrics made with hot iron on the brows of those whom they let out of their concentration camps.

"I be lookin' for someun called Dikar," the man mumbled, peering. Deep within his eyes a glow smoldered like that which shows in the ashes of a dying fire.

"I am Dikar."

"Yeh be? Then I'm ter take yeh ter th' Commissary. He needs yeh."

"He needs—" Dikar looked at Marilee, muttered, "It would be funny if you turned out to be right." Then he was saying to the stooped-over man, "Come on. What are we waitin' for?"

In a little while, Dikar was striding back in again through the arched doorway of the house that had been given the Bunch to live in, and he was smiling as he had not smiled since the morning after the fight that took West Point.

Noise met him in the narrow, stone-lined, stone-floored passage, laughing cries of young voices and a quick pat-pat of running bare feet on stone; and then he was in the big, sunny room that was between the room where the Boys slept and the one where the Girls slept. A slight, beardless youngster darted in and out among the tables and chairs, dodging a red-bearded bigger Boy who doggedly chased him.

"Go it, Carlberger," the other youngsters shrilled, and deeper voices yelled, "Get him, Timohare. Grab him!" choking with laughter. The Girls, brown-limbed and sparkling-eyed, impartially cheered both or gave tiny squeals of alarm as Timohare crashed into a chair Carlberger threw in his way, or Carlberger twisted just in time to escape Timohare's clutching fingers.

The youngster jumped on a long table, jumped down on the other side. Timohare stopped, panted, "I'll wring your little neck, you rabbit. I'll teach you not to sneak up an' stuff prickleburrs down the back of my fawn-skin."

"Sticks an' stones," Carlberger chanted, thumbing his nose, "may break my bones, but words will never hurt." A sudden vault took Timohare clear over the table, and he had his tormentor in his big-pawed grip.

"Fins," the youngster gurgled. "Fins, Timohare. I promise I won't do it again."

"You betcha you won't," the bigger Boy grunted. "Not when I get through with—"

"Hold it!" Dikar called. "Hold it, you two. Come here, all you Boys, I've got somethin to tell you."

THE LAUGHING and the yelling stopped all of a sudden, and there was only the sound of feet as the Boys gathered eagerly around Dikar. The Girls crowded up behind the Boys, their long-lashed eyes anxious.

"What is it, Dikar?" Marilee asked, low-voiced, somehow alongside him "What's happened?"

"You'll hear in a minute." His arm slid across her shoulders, and then he was talking to the Bunch. "Listen, fellows," he was saying. "I was just called to the Commissary, the man Normanfenton has put in charge of givin' out food to all the people here in West Point. He told me that there's hardly any food left. With so many people crowdin' in here, most of the Asafrics' store is used up already."

"Phew-w-w," someone whistled. "That's nice." Johnstone it was, thin, his square jaw darkly stubbled. "That's very nice."

"The Quartermaster," Dikar went on, "has put it up to us to get more. Over beyond the hill behind this row of houses and past the woods other side of it, there are a lot of cows, those animals like fat, clumsy deer with un-branched horns that these people kill an' eat."

"Dikar!" Marilee interrupted. "That's way outside the line of pillboxes."

"Right," Dikar smiled tightly. "It's way outside the fort, so if anyone goes out to get those cows an' is attacked by the Asafrics, the big guns couldn't protect 'em because they'd shoot our men as well as the blacks.

"Besides, the cows can't be driven to the fort because they'd have to be driven through the woods, and they're so full of brambles an' thorny bushes the cows won't go that way. That means they have to be killed right out there an' cut up an' carried in.

"Now, if a bunch of men was sent out with rifles to shoot 'em, the sound of the firin' would surely bring any Asafrics that are skulkin' around. It's all got to be done very quiet, an' that's where we come in. Our arrows don't make any sound—"

"Hurray!" Carlberger yelled. "That's goin' to be fun. Let's—"

"Wait," Dikar snapped. "Wait a minute an' listen to me. It won't be fun. If we're spotted out there by the Asafrics, we'll stay out there, dead. That's why the Commissary didn't order me to take you Boys out there, only asked me, and that's why I'm only askin' you to come with me, not orderin' you. I don't want anyone to come unless he really wants to. Now. Who's comin'?"

He stopped talking. Feet shuffled, and there was a hiss of indrawn breath, but nobody said anything. Not for a long minute.

Then Timohare, grinning no longer, said very quietly: "We're all comin', Dikar. You knew that. You didn't have to ask."

"I knew you all would," Dikar smiled. "But I had to ask. All right, fellows. Get your bonarrers an' your knives an' let's get started."

THE OTHER side of the hill was all tall grass; there were no trees. Up out of the grass, midslope of the hill, rose half-balls of dirty-white stone each big enough to hold four or five men. There were men in each of these pillboxes, and guns that could lay down on the grassy hillside a chattering hailstorm of death.

A gentle wind rustled the tall grasses sloping down from the pillboxes to the edge of the woods that made shadowy the foot of the hill. The grasses moved scarcely more than they had moved all day in the soft breeze, but all of a sudden a new shadow glided among the shadows just within the edge of the woods. It was a lithe-limbed Boy who had crept there down the slope of the hill.

Another Boy appeared, and another, till eighteen of them were gathering around Dikar, and so silent were they that a rabbit nibbling a tender green shoot not ten paces away was not disturbed at all.

The Boys had left behind their fawn-skins, were naked except for their little twig-aprons, but they had their bows, and their quivers of arrows hung from their shoulders, and their sharp hunting knives were in their belts.

"You each know the number I gave you before I started," Dikar murmured. "I'll go ahead a little. If everything's all right I'll point to the cows, one after the other, an' Number One will aim at the first one I point to, Number Two at the second, and so on, but you won't shoot till I lift my arm above my head, and then you'll shoot all together. Everyone understand?"

He looked at each one in turn, and each one nodded. He turned to the gray trunk of the tree under which he stood, lifted his arms and sprang.

Leaves rustled. The rabbit flipped his stub of a tail, looked around. Only the tree trunks and the dappled shadows of the foliage were between him and the sun and the tall grasses beyond the edge of the woods.

Dikar ran easily through the tops of the trees, leaped from the swaying bough to bough as easily as though he ran on firm ground. The green smells of the leaves were in his nostrils, the sharper smell of tree bark, and dark, damp smell of the ground beneath. No man smell, no man sound, came to him. He might have been in the woods on the Mountain, the two nights and days just past only a dreadful dream from which he had wakened.

The treetops were suddenly brighter ahead of Dikar and blue sky was shining through. He stopped and crouched on a thick limb, and peered out of the woods and down into a rolling, flower-dotted field.

Brown of body, white-faced, the ungainly beasts of the Far Land that were called *cows* cropped grass everywhere in the field or drank noisily from a little stream that wandered through it. A low wall of tumbled stone closed off one end of the field, the stream running under it, and beyond the wall Dikar could see another field of tall yellow grass rippling in the breeze. It sloped gently up and over the top of a low hill.

The woods curved around the other end of the cows' field till it came to the low wall of tumbled stone and swallowed this and ran on up the hill. The breeze came across the field to Dikar. He sniffed it, his nostrils wide, his eyes half-closed, the corner of his mouth twitching. There was only the smell of the woods in the breeze, and the smells of the flowers and the cows, and a faint tang of wood-smoke.

Dikar swung down to the ground, took two or three steps into the field. He felt the eyes of the Boys upon him, though there was no hint in sound or sight that they were in the tree-tops, watching him.

A COW lifted its head, looked at him with great, friendly eyes, its jaws moving from side to side, greenish spit dribbling from the corner of its mouth. Dikar pointed at it, pointed at the one next to it, at one lying down. He pointed at fourteen cows; there were no more.

That was fine. When one of them had been skinned, its head and legs cut off and its insides cleaned out, as he'd told the Bunch to do, it would be no heavier than a grown deer. Each of the bigger Boys could carry a deer on his, shoulders, but Dikar had been worried about the weaker youngsters. Now eight of the kids would only have to carry half a cow apiece.

Dikar lifted his arm above his head. Bowstrings twanged in the treetops and arrows zipped across the field, almost too fast for the eye to follow. Cows thudded down, all the cows, an arrow in the eye of one, in the flank of another, in the breast of a third. Brown Boys dropped down out of the trees, darted to the dead cows, knives flashing.

It had all been done almost without a sound, certainly without any sound that could have been heard a hundred paces away, but Dikar suddenly was uneasy.

Carlberger ran up to him. "You didn't point out one for me." The youngster sounded as if he was ready to bawl. "I was number eighteen an' so I didn't get a chance to shoot."

"I'm sorry, kid." Dikar put his arm around the Boy's shoulder. "There just weren't enough to go around, but I'll see that you're Number One next time, so you'll surely get a chance."

A queer prickle was running up and down his back and his hair was tightening on the top of his head. "Look. You take care of somethin' for me. I'm goin' into the woods a ways, so tell Johnstone to take charge. Tell him an' everyone that if they hear a crow caw in the woods three times, they're to drop what they're doin' quick an' get up into the treetops an' wait to hear from me."

"Dikar!" Carlberger stared at him, round-eyed. "You don't think the Asafrics—"

"No," Dikar grinned. "I just think we ought to take care. We're awful far from the fort, you know. Now run along and do what I said."

Carlberger ran off and Dikar turned back to the woods, and his grin was gone. As he went up again into the treetop out of which he had dropped, he had found out what was bothering him.

The direction of the wind had changed a little and it was faintly tainted with the smell of an Asafric.

Dikar moved into the wind now, more silently even than before, in the same direction as the nearer edge of the field ran and toward where the woods curved around it. The smell was still faint, but it was growing stronger, ever so little. Now there was another smell, a man smell, but not the smell of an Asafric.

So there were two.

The leaf shadows deepened about Dikar, so that he knew he had passed the end of the field where the cows were. He kept going. Then he flattened suddenly along the bough he was on, making himself a part of it.

He'd heard a murmur of voices in the green brush, below and ahead of him. Now that he'd stopped moving he made out words. "Yoh be big fella careful." The thick-mouthed voice of an Asafric Black. "Yoh not let rebels cotch yoh gettin' back inside fo't." And then he heard a rustle of movement in the bushes.

The smell of the Asafric and the smell of the white separated, trailing on the wind from different directions. The white was going away through the bushes, toward the fort.

He was a spy on the Americans inside the fort, had met the Asafric here to tell him what was going on in West Point, was going back to find out more. Dikar had to see who he was. He started moving toward that rustle in the bushes, very fast.

So fast that he stepped on a rotten limb, started falling, snatched at another to save himself. "Who dar?" a startled cry burst out beneath him. "Who dat?" And then the thick-mouthed voice was grunting, "Ah see yoh!"

It was too late to escape.

Dikar saw a black hand lifting out of the green brush, a little gun in it lifting to aim at him.

CHAPTER 3
SALUTE THE PRESIDENT

GUN CRASH was loud in the hush of the woods. A brown body hurtled down out of the tall tree, pounded the Asafric to the ground. Someone shouted. Underbrush threshed about the two tossing bodies, brown and naked, black and green-uniformed.

Dikar's strong fingers clamped a black wrist. That hand clutched the gun; the black's first bullet had missed Dikar. Plunging down, Dikar had snatched his knife from his belt, but now the Asafric seized his arm, and a green-clothed knee dug into his chest, pinned him down on the ground.

Foul breath stank in Dikar's face. Tiny, animal-like eyes glared down at him. The purplish lips twisted, said thickly, "Yoh one big fella fool try fight Jubal. Jubal not kill you now. Yoh strong, not die quick, but yoh wish youse'f daid befoh Cap'n Tsi Huan get t'rough wid yoh."

"You'll have to take me to him first," Dikar grunted. "Think you can?"

"Know I can." The Boys in the field would hear Dikar if he cried for help, but there might be other blacks near. They could be as quiet in the woods as the Boys. His call might bring them too. "Jubal neber see no 'Merican he no can han'le."

"Here's one!" Dikar heaved up, tore his knife-hand free, slashed the blade across the black throat, all in one sudden, irresistible movement. Blood gushed out over Dikar and the Asafric rolled off of him, was very still on the ground.

Dikar was on his feet, breath clamped in his throat, all his nerves strained for sight or smell or sound of other Asafrics.

The silence of the woods closed about him, a hush alive with leaf-rustle, with the buzz of insects, the peeping of birds and the *whirr* of their wings, but empty of all human noises. Even the white spy was already too far away to be heard.

Lids half-closed, Dikar's blue eyes roamed the brush, found a bent twig, a brushed bit of moss. Dikar got moving, and where he passed there were no bent twigs, not even a leaf turned wrongside out, to tell which way he had gone.

The trail of the spy went toward the fort, and to Dikar it was as broad and plain as though it were the stone-paved path that circled the Plain. He followed it swiftly, till he came to the stream that he had seen curving across the fields where the cows were, and there it ended.

Dikar's quarry had waded up or down in the water, and there were trees leaning across by way of which he might have left it. If he knew woodcraft at all it would take hours to find where, and by that time he would be back in the fort and his spoor would be mixed with all the many others. Most likely he was a Beast Man, Dikar thought, to be so apt in the ways of the woods.

He washed himself in the stream, washed his knife, and went back to the field. The Boys had finished their butchering and were ready to start lugging the great red and white loads of meats back to West Point.

DIKAR WENT ahead to find a path for them through the thorn-choked, woods, tight with watchfulness till at last they were all over the hill and safely past the line of pillboxes. Then he sped across the Plain to find Normanfenton and tell him about the spy.

"The pattern holds," the leader sighed. "Two centuries ago West Point had its Benedict Arnold, and now— Thanks, my boy," he broke off. "I shall have Walt warn the outposts to keep a sharper watch from now on, and to do what he can to track down the spy, but I fear, what with all the strangers here, that it will be almost impossible."

It seemed to Dikar that his story had touched only the surface of Normanfenton's mind, that other matters filled it more deeply. "By the way, Dikar," the older man went on. "In half an hour I want you to be at Headquarters."

The room called Headquarters was very big and its roof, of dark wood laid on huge, rough-axed beams, very high, but even though the late afternoon sun came in through a window that took up all one end of it, it was dim as the deeps of the Mountain's forest.

Coming into it, Dikar decided this was because the wood of the walls swallowed the sunlight in their quiet, dark glow, and because the ragged flags hanging from poles that stuck straight out from the walls, high up, threw slow-swaying shadows over the long, heavy table that ran down the room's middle, and over the men who sat around it.

"You're the last, son," Normanfenton said from the end of the table. As he pointed to an empty chair, his sleeve pulled back and uncovered the scabby ring on his wrist where the Asafric's iron cuff had rubbed raw the prisoner's flesh.

Dikar went to the chair, the thick stuff that was laid over the floor tickling the bare soles of his feet, and sat down. Johndawson was on one side of him, the gray-haired, thin man with old pain lined into his face who was the first of the people from the Far Land that Dikar brought to the Mountain.

The only other man here whom Dikar had known before he came to West Point was Walt, who sat up there next to Normanfenton, making marks on a paper with a round little stick.

Dikar knew the marks Walt was making had a meaning, but he did not know how to make out the meaning. The marks were called writing, and making out their meaning was reading.

A narrow-faced, pale man across the table asked, "Are we ready to begin, now, General?" That was what they all called Normanfenton. It meant the same as Boss. "We're anxious to hear what you have on your mind." His name was Paine. He wasn't one of the Beast Folk who had helped to take West Point, but had come here the morning after the fight, from a place called Newburg. "Do you mind telling us?"

"I don't mind at all." Normanfenton's slow, sad smile stole over his face. "Since that is why I called you together." Of the three others in the room, the one called Morgan was the leader of the Beast Folk, while Holton and Gary were farmers who had joined up later, like Paine.

"Colonel Dawson has finally got in communication with the Secret Net, that league of devoted patriots who for all these years have worked in constant peril of torture and death to keep alive some small measure of resistance to the Asafrics.

"It is because of them that America still lives in the hearts of men, and the secret radio network they operate is the authentic voice of that America."

"We know all that," Paine growled. "What's the idea of making a speech about it?"

"You will find out soon. But first I want you to hear what we have learned. John, please."

JOHNDAWSON FUMBLED with a paper on the table in front of him. "Word of what we've done here," he began, "has spread through the country like wildfire. I've been talking with National Prime himself, the anonymous chief of the Net, and I give you my word, gentlemen, that the very dots and dashes his hand hammered out crackled with his joy and excitement.

"There is new hope in the land, my friends—this land that hasn't known hope for more than a decade. There is a new spirit of defiance."

He stopped, shrugged shoulders scrawny even in the new gray-blue that covered them. "What I've learned has me so worked up myself, that I'm making a speech. It amounts to this. Our people everywhere, inspired by our example, are rising against the Asafrics.

"The workers in a Nevada silver mine bashed in the heads of their guards and have barricaded themselves underground, sworn to die rather than surrender. In Seattle, longshoremen set fire to a half-dozen ships loaded with lumber for the Orient and fought off the black soldiers till the cargoes were altogether destroyed.

"A riot has started in Chicago and is still going on in spite of the machine guns with which the Asafrics are mowing down the mob. In Pittsburgh—"

"For the love of God, man!" Gary broke in, "you don't think that sort of thing's good news, do you?" He was grizzled, hollow-cheeked, stooped under a weight of toil and sorrow. "Those poor damn fools won't get anywhere that way. They'll be murdered by the Asafrics, and that will be the end of everything. It's got to stop. We've got to stop them, somehow."

"You are right, of course," Normanfenton said quietly. "These unarmed, unorganized outbreaks will be quickly and ruthlessly put down, and will have accomplished nothing. I have already instructed National Prime to have the operatives of his Net quiet the people of their districts and then set about organizing them into semi-military bodies, prepared to act as and how we shall direct."

"Just a minute, General," Paine, drawled. "What makes you think anyone is going to do as you instruct?"

Normanfenton's deepset, somber eyes moved to him. "Your question is very much to the point, Captain Paine. I shall ask Colonel Dawson to answer it."

Everyone looked at Johndawson. He picked up a paper from the table, and Dikar saw that his bony hand was shaking a little. "This," he said, "is the first message I received from National Prime. It is addressed to General Fenton.

"It says: 'Upon learning of your exploit and pending establishment of communication with you, I have had operatives of Secret Net reach all Americans possible to reach. I now have reports speaking for all sections of country. They unanimously authorize me to request that you assume Provisional Presidency of New America born today, and appoint whomever you may select as Provisional Congress.

" 'I am further authorized to pledge loyalty of all patriots, their obedience to your proclamations and laws of your Congress, until the battle now beginning ends in victory or annihilation. Every American joins in prayer that you and the Second Continental Congress will lead us anew to the freedom that our forefathers of First wrested from other tyrants two hundred seven years ago. Signed: National Prime, for the People of the United States.' "

JOHNDAWSON'S VOICE rang out clear in the dim hush of the flag-hung room, thrilling even Dikar, who had understood very little of what he was reading. And then for a long time no one moved, no one made a sound.

Though there was no wind, it seemed to Dikar that one of the flags, a faded old one with a picture of a coiled snake on its tattered folds, fluttered as if ghostly hands were waving it over Normanfenton's massive head.

A murmur went through the room, like the murmur of the dawn wind in the trees, and the room awoke as the forest awakes in the dawn.

"You've accepted, of course," Holton said, a small man with tight, thin lips and eyes like two polished stones. "It's a great honor, General, and—"

"I've accepted." Normanfenton's head lifted. "But it is less honor than a heavy burden that has been laid upon me. I have asked my Maker to give me the strength to bear it, and it would be well, I think, that you gentlemen also appeal to Him for strength and wisdom, for I am constituting you the Second Continental Congress of the United States of America...."

"No!" He put up his hand to stop the words that were springing to the lips of his hearers. "No talk, please, and no meaningless ceremony. We must get to work at once. The plane that flew over us this afternoon was only one warning that the enemy is gathering his forces to move against us."

"Only one!" Gary exclaimed, sharply. "It's clear enough them flyers was sent to spy out how strong we are, but what else has happened?"

"It is more what has *not* happened that is ominous. From National Prime we learn that he has heard nothing from the Net's agents in the region bounded roughly by the Delaware and Housatonic Rivers on the west and east, north by a line drawn through Kingston, south by one through New York."

"We're just about in the center of that."

"Exactly. Somehow, the Asafrics have succeeded in silencing all the Net's secret radio stations in exactly the territory through which they must come to attack us."

"Another thing, General," Walt spoke for the first time. "There have been no newcomers in camp since dark. The last one has had to dodge some of the enemy's armored scout cars."

"Jehosaphat!" Holton's hand slapped down on the table. "The men in my company who were on duty in the pillboxes last night thought they heard firing in the distance. Since we have no patrols out, I paid very little attention—"

"Hold on!" Gary interrupted. "I saw— Look here. Me an' my boys was on the roofs standin' by the anti-aircraft guns. The sky was kind of red, all around the horizon, like as if there was some big fires burnin'."

"Yes." A sort of grayness was spreading under Normanfenton's skin. "Yes. Knowing Viceroy Yee Hashomoto's usual procedure in dealing with any defiance of his authority, we can come pretty close to guessing what the Asafrics are about. I—"

"Not me." Morgan's face was almost black, the look in his narrowed eyes frightening. "I don't have ter guess. I saw 'em do it ter my—our little town uh Cornwall th' night I split open th' head of th' yaller dog thet drug off my Janey.

"Hidin' out on Storm King, I saw 'em whup ter death every tenth white man in town an' ship all th' rest, an' every woman an' child fer a mile aroun', off God knows whar, arter fust makin' 'em set fire ter their own houses. That's whut they're doin' now, from Esopus Crick ter th' Narrows, ter get even fer whut we done here."

"There can be no doubt of that," Paine murmured, half-smiling. "You should have known that would happen when you started this. If you sow the wind, you must expect to reap the whirlwind."

Gary twisted around to him. "It don't seem to be botherin' you none, *Captain* Paine." His voice was a growl in his throat. "No more'n if you was a Mudskin."

MEN LOOKED swiftly to the two, muscles twitched in startled faces. Dikar knew why this was. Mudskin was the Far Land name for yellow-bellied whites who knuckled under to the Asafrics and did their dirty work, and so it was a fighting name that Gary had called Paine.

But nothing happened. Paine just kept smiling, said smooth-ly, "I don't think you really mean that, Gary." Dikar noticed that his pale eyes were not smiling. "In case you do, may I point out that if I were a renegade I should hardly have hastened here to volunteer my services."

"Mebbe not," Gary growled. "Or mebee you was sent here to spy on us." Spy! Could Paine be the spy who'd met Jubal in the woods? "It would be kind of nice for the Asafrics if they knew our plans quick as we know them ourselves." There was no way for Dikar to tell, he hadn't seen the spy, hadn't heard his voice.

"Have you any proof of that accusation?" Two white spots had blossomed either side of Paine's thin nose. "If—"

"Course I ain't got proof. How kin I? But I promise you right now I'm goin' to watch you every minute from now on, an' if I ketch you steppin' off the straight an' narrow by so much as an inch—"

"Mr. Gary!" Normanfenton's face was black as his beard. "Captain Paine!" His eyes flashed lightnings. "I want this stopped at once. We're not a bunch of boys here, squabbling over some childish game. We are men who have undertaken the responsibility of leading a people.

"If we waste ourselves in petty bickering we are as much traitors to that people as any Mudskin. If we do not trust one another, how can we be worthy of the trust of others. If we cannot govern ourselves, how can we expect to govern a nation? We will have no more of that sort of thing…. Our first business—"

"Look, Normanfenton," Dikar interrupted. "Before you get started, I want to say somethin."

"What is it, son?"

"I don't belong here." Dikar pushed himself up out of his chair, swallowed and went on. "Somethin you just said shows me that. You—you said that we're not a bunch of boys here. Well, I am a Boy."

He knew what it was he had to say, but it was hard to know how to say it. "Maybe I'm not much younger than Walt there, but all I know about anythin' is what the Mountain has taught me, the ways of the green growin' things, the ways of the birds an' the rabbits an' the deer.

"I love America as much as any of you, but I am not fit to be one of its Bosses. I thank you for askin' me to be here, but I should only be in the way if I stay an' so I am not stayin'."

Dikar was going away from the table. He was going across the room to the door and voices behind him were saying things but he did not understand what they said. He went out of the door and closed it behind him and he felt awful bad.

Dikar felt bad because he knew that the names of those in that room would be remembered in this land long after they were all dead, and now his name would not be among them.

CHAPTER 4

PERIL FOR A PATRIOT

BACK IN the House of the Bunch, Dikar told Marilee what he had done, and she said he had done right.

"On the Mountain," Marilee said, "every mornin' after Brekfes, you would tell us what jobs were to be done that day, and to do each job you would pick the one who could do that job best. An' at Evenin' Council, it was not *what* a Boy or Girl had done, whether choppin' wood or washin' dishes, or bossin' some big job, that brought them praise or blame from the Bunch, but *how* they had done it.

"Now you keep sayin' that the ways of this Far Land are different from our ways on the Mountain, but I cannot believe that in this the way of the Far Land is different.

"When your last Evenin' Council is over, Dikar, an' you are sleepin' your last sleep, it will not be havin' your name remembered by those who live after you that will matter, but whether you will have done as best you could the job you could do best, whether that job was a big one or a little."

And then Marilee went back to helping the other Girls get Supper ready, but Dikar felt a lot better.

It started to get dark, so Dikar pulled down black cloths over all the windows and went to the wall and pushed a little button that stuck out of the wall. He jumped a little as all the bulbs in the roof filled with light, and a great "Ah-h-h" came from the Bunch, but their eyes widened.

This was a magic that still frightened them a little, though Walt had showed them, in a building down by the River, great wheels turned by a downrushing waterfall and told them that the wheels were making a something called electricity that filled the bulbs with light and did other wonderful things.

Just as supper was finished and the Girls were starting to

clear the tables, Walt came into the room. Dikar went to him, smiling welcome. "We are going to have a sing, Walt, like we used to around the Fire under the great Oak in the Clearin'. It will be nice to have you sing with us."

"Some other time, Dikar." Walt's answering smile was grave, his eyes shadowed. "Tonight... But you'd better come outside with me, where we can talk without being overheard."

Outside the House it was very dark, because it was an order that the black cloths be pulled down over all the windows in the buildings at night and that no one show a light where it could be seen from the sky. In the sky, of course, were the stars, but they were high up and far away and all around the black hills crouched, the hills over which at any moment might come the terrible planes of the Asafrics.

"Listen, fellow." Walt put his arm around Dikar's shoulder. "I've been sent to ask you whether you're willing to attempt something the chance against whose success is a thousand to one, and failure in which means death or worse."

"It is for the Cause?"

"Naturally."

"Tell me," Dikar said softly, "what it is I am to do."

Walt's arm tightened on his shoulder, fell away. "Come. I have something to show you. I'll explain on the way."

THEY STARTED walking across the Plain. "We have decided that the Asafrics have so far left us alone only because they are busy putting down the people's uprisings all over the country.

"By cooling our heels here till they are free again to concentrate a strong force against us, we are playing into their hands. If what we've done is not to peter out into just another futile foray, we've got to make a move very soon."

"Yes. But what can we do?"

"We can strike, swiftly and unexpectedly, where we can do a lot of damage and return to the comparative safety of this fort before they recover from their surprise and cut off our retreat. This will sting them into withdrawing troops from other sectors in order to attack us in force.

"Thanks to what their engineers have accomplished here, we can stand a long siege. While it is going on, our people will attack the strong points whose garrisons have been weakened, overwhelm them, and use them as bases for other raids similar to ours. That will either relieve the pressure on West Point, or compel Yee Hashamoto to weaken other strong points, further away, where the same tactics will be repeated.

"In this way the rebellion will spread, like ripples from a stone thrown into a pond, all over the country, and there is a chance that before reinforcements can arrive from their home-land we can defeat the Asafric Army of Occupation and drive it into the seas. A slim chance, but a chance, nevertheless."

"That's grand!" Dikar exclaimed. They'd reached the other side of the Plain but instead of going into one of the buildings there, Walt was guiding him through a space between two of them. "It's a grand plan."

"It is the best we could work out." Beyond the buildings, bush-covered ground fell steeply down toward the River. "But it depends entirely on the success of our first raid." They started clambering down through the rustling dark. "We can't go wandering around aimlessly looking for Asafrics to fight, nor dare we risk tackling a force so strong that we'll be defeated or so many of us killed that we can no longer hope to hold West Point. We've got to know exactly where to go, what we'll find when we get there. That's what we need you for."

Through the bushes, starlight glinted on black water. "You want me to go out and look for—"

"No." The ground leveled out, became the road that ran along the River. "What we want you to do is more dangerous even than that."

Walt's hand on Dikar's elbow turned him so that they were going along the road. A little ahead, a blacker bulk against the black was a little House between the road and the River. "Dikar, since you've been in West Point, you must have heard a lot about Benjamin Apgar."

"I sure have," Dikar growled. "They say he's the worst Mudskin of them all."

"A white man who cast in his lot with the invaders," Walt agreed, "almost before their conquest was completed, who toadied and licked boots, and made himself so valuable to them that Hashamoto commissioned him a major and put him on his personal staff. Execrated, reviled through the length and breadth of America as its foulest renegade—Benjamin Apgar is perhaps its most devoted patriot."

"Huh!" Dikar stopped stockstill in front of the little House. "He's *what?*"

"You're no more astonished than we were when we radioed National Prime for advice and he told us that Apgar for years had been acting as a super-spy for the Secret Net. He's saved countless lives—but you can figure out yourself how much he could do, in the Viceroy's confidence, constantly at Headquarters in New York."

The road had been cut into the hill here, so a high, steep earth bank made it velvet black, but Dikar could hear that Walt was fumbling at the door of the little House. "Major Apgar can tell us what we need to know, and he's the only one who can, but Z3, the station through which he communicated with the Net, is one of those that has been silenced. We've got to reach him. You've got to reach him, Dikar, and get the dope from him, and get it back to us."

A CREAK of hinges, a gust of warm air thick with the smell of the armored trucks they had captured from the Asafrics, told Dikar the door was opening.

"Come on in," Walt said and rough wood sagged under Dikar's weight as he obeyed. "You will have to go into the city, into Asafric Headquarters, teeming with enemies. Death, certain but not quick, will be the price of discovery." The door closed behind them. "We all volunteered to attempt it, but General Fenton decided that you were the best bet to pull it off."

"Me?" Dikar was puzzled. "Why me?"

A click. Sudden light blinded him. "Your skin is as brown," Walt's voice came out of the dazzle, "as that of certain Asafrics, not true Blacks but a race called Abyssinians who are supposed to be descendants of the lost tribes of Israel."

Dikar's eyes cleared. The floor of the room ended abruptly, and beyond was water, closed off by a wall that was a big door. The truck-smell came from a big hollow something that floated in the black and greasy water. "You can easily pass as one of them." Walt went on, "except for your blond hair and beard—they wear beards, luckily—and I've got dye here to take care of that."

Walt took a bottle and a little brush from a bench near the door. Dikar saw a green Asafric uniform lying on the bench. "Even if I look like an Ab-Abyss—what you said—I can't talk like one. They'll know I'm a faker as soon as I open my mouth."

"No." Walt opened the bottle, poured black stuff from it on the brush. "The Abyssinians talk a different language from the other Blacks, and so to the yellow officers they use pidgin English. You've listened to our prisoners enough to imitate that, haven't you?"

"Me t'ink so." Dikar made his voice come out of the back of his throat. "Me good mak' talk lak black fella boy." He grinned delightedly at his success. "W'at yoh say, 'Merican?"

"You'll do." Walt grinned back, starting to brush the black stuff into Dikar's hair. "Especially when you get into that uniform. What a time I had finding a prisoner big enough for his clothes to fit you! Yes, you'll do, unless you run into a real Abyssinian and they're so few there's little danger of that.

"Now here's the plan: (Lift your head so I can get at the underside of your beard.) Gary's meeting us here in a few minutes and he'll run you down the River in that motorboat." Walt pointed to the big thing in the water. "He'll try to get you to the ruins of Yonkers unobserved, land you there and hang around to pick you up, but it's too much to hope that things will go as smoothly as that.

"If you're stopped by a river patrol, you'll have a pass with you—Paine's faking one now on one of the Army forms we found here—that ought to take care of you, and you'll say that Gary's a deserter with valuable information for Major Apgar's ears alone; you'll insist on being taken to him.

"If you do manage to get to land before you run into any Asafrics, you'll pull the same story, except that it will be you who will have the important information that can only be told to Apgar. After that—well after that, you'll have to depend on Apgar to get you out of New York.

"All right. That's all I can do. It's a good job, if I do say so myself. Now get into that uniform."

Dikar sat down on the bench, got all tangled up in the green cloth. Walt helped him, said, "Good thing a lot of the Asafrics don't wear shoes, so you can get away with going barefoot. Otherwise the clumsy way you'd walk would give you away. You sure you understand what you're to do?"

"I understand," Dikar answered, standing up. He felt all bound up, uncomfortable. "Look, Walt. If I don't come back, will you tell Johnstone to be Boss of the Bunch? An'—an' tell Marilee I tried my best to do the thing I was best fitted for, an' that I was happy to have the chance to try."

"I won't have to tell her anything," Walt said, but Dikar could see by the look on his face that wasn't what he was thinking. "You'll do all the telling yourself, when you come back…. Gary ought to be here by now. Wonder what's keeping him. I'd better take a look outside."

He touched a button in the wall next to the door. Sightless darkness swallowed him, the room.

Hinges creaked. The darkness paled, where the sound came from. The green smell of outdoors was in Dikar's nostrils, the cool night wind. Somewhere above, not far away, the bushes threshed loudly.

"Here he is," Walt said. Then Dikar was suddenly alert. There was a dull, crunching sound up there. A curious gurgle ended abruptly. Light leaped out from something in Walt's hand, a slender shaft of light. It struck the steep leafy bank, caught in its brightness a sprawling black thing that came over the top of the bank and fell, and thudded on the road below.

The crumpled heap did not move. Dikar saw a face, bloody, misshapen. Gary's face! It was Gary who lay there, and the top of his head was crushed in by some terrific blow.

CHAPTER 5
MAGICAL CITY

DIKAR SHOVED Walt out of his way, darted past the body in the road, leaped at the bank and clawed up; hands, feet, finding hold by instinct. The bushes above were loud with the noise of someone running away.

Dikar got to the top, twisted toward the sounds; a red streak jetted across the night and shot-sound banged in Dikar's ears. He threw himself at the black figure the light-flash showed him. His shoulder pounded into a form that went down and he went down on top of it, his knees finding a body, crunching it into the ground, his fingers finding a flailing arm, clutching it.

"Got you," he grunted. "Give up or I'll tear you to little pieces."

The man under him went limp. "Dikar!" It was Paine's voice. "Get off me, Dikar. I've got to see if I've winged him."

"Him?" Gary was right. Paine was a Mudskin. An Asafric spy. "What are you try in to put over on me?" Gary had tumbled to Paine, had said he was going to watch him, so Paine killed him. "What 'him' are you babblin' about?"

"The one who murdered—God, man! You don't think *I* did that!"

"Didn't you?"

"No, damn you. I—" All of a sudden there was light on Paine, on the dead leaves under him. Walt was standing over them and the light came from the thing he held, and he was looking, sidewise, at something to which he moved the light.

It was a man lying across a bush. His hands were clutched to his breast and they were red with the stain that spread in the gray-blue cloth under them.

Walt's light moved up a little. Eyes, open but sightless, stared out of a knobby, rock-jawed face. "Morgan, eh!" Paine exclaimed. "Buck Morgan! I saw him silhouetted against the sky, clubbing Gary."

Walt bent, picked up something. Dikar shoved himself up off Paine. Walt said, "How did you happen to see that, Paine? How did you happen to be down here to see it?"

Paine held up a hand and Dikar pulled him to his feet. "I didn't have the pass quite ready when Gary came to my quarters to get it, so I told him to go on down and make his final arrangements with you and I'd bring it in a couple minutes.

"I wasn't much longer than that, but I was just too long, because I was only in time to see the murder, outlined against the stars. Morgan must have heard me, because he started to run. "I slanted to meet him, shot—and then Dikar hit me like a ton of coal. Buck Morgan's the last one I'd have thought to be a renegade."

Dikar recalled how, in the woods, he'd decided that the spy was a Beast Man, on account of the way he covered his trail.

"This is his revolver, then," Walt was saying, holding out what he'd picked up from the ground. Its handle was bloody, hairs stuck to it. "He clubbed Gary with its butt. But I can't understand why. It would have been smarter to let Dikar accomplish his mission if he could, tip off the Asafrics to ambush us on our way to the raid so they could wipe us out."

"He couldn't take a chance on being able to reach them," Paine broke in, "with the outposts on the watch for him after Dikar's warning. Besides— Wait! Here's what he was up to.

"I saw him deliberately shove Gary over the bank. He expected to pick you and Dikar off as you heard the fall and came out of the boathouse. Then he'd grab the motorboat, shoot down to New York, and expose Apgar. That one piece of information would fix him well with Hashamoto, and he wouldn't have to risk his neck here any longer."

"Sounds reasonable.... There's your gun." Walt pointed past the bush. "Dikar must have hit you like a charging bull to have sent it flying that far."

"I'll say he did." Paine hobbled over, picked it up. "But we're wasting time. Dikar's got to get started soon or it will be daylight before he gets down-river."

"Right!" Walt snapped. "Let's get going." He started leading them back the way he'd come up, around the steeper part of the bank. "With Gary gone, I'll have to go with him, and—"

Paine shook his head. "It's a hundred-to-one bet against Dikar's getting back safely, but that's a dead sure thing compared to the chances of the one who goes with him. Apgar won't dare free a deserter, even if that bluff goes over. Therefore, friend Walt, I'm the one to go."

"No—"

"Walt!" Dikar interrupted, feeling proud he was an American as he heard these two quarrel about who should die for the Cause. "Listen, Walt. You're Normanfenton's best helper. He needs you here. As long as someone has to go with me, it has to be Captain Paine."

"I guess you're right," Walt sighed. Then, looking at Paine, "Do you know the River?"

"I know the River."

THE RIVER was as wide and empty as the sky, and Dikar could tell where River left off and sky began only by the black crouch of the hills between them. Stars sprinkled the sky with tiny lights, sprinkled the River, but there were no lights on the land, nothing to show that anyone lived there or ever had lived there.

The wind carried the smells of the land to Dikar, the green smells of grass and trees, the dark brown smells of earth—a smell of wood burned, of the cold ashes of homes the Asafrics had burned down.

Dikar stared at the blackness that was the land till his eyes ached. The boat purred down the River, very quietly, and the lap of water against the sides of the boat was a quiet sound. In a while Dikar's eyelids closed. He drowsed and woke, and nothing was changed, not sky nor River nor black crouch of the hills, nor the still shape of Paine hunched silent over a little wheel in the front of the boat. Dikar's eyes closed again, and he slept.

And sleeping, Dikar shivered with chill. He stirred and awoke, and he was lying face up to the sky. The sky was no longer black but gray, the stars faded.

He lifted. Paine was no longer a black, still shape in the front of the boat, but a man in blue-gray only a little darker than the sky. The chill that had waked Dikar was the dawn-wind, and the River was paling with the dawn. "Paine!" Dikar exclaimed. "Captain Paine! I thought you were going to put me on land before it got light!" Paine's head turned, his face narrow in the dawn-light, his eyes burning. "I fell asleep at the wheel," he said, thin-lipped. "And when I woke up, I saw—" He gestured out over the water.

There were other boats on the water, little ones and boats unbelievably huge. The Asafrics in them looked at Dikar's boat and looked away. "There was nothing left except to brazen it out," Paine said, despair in his voice. "Nothing left except to run down to a pier in the heart of the city and try to get away with our story that I'm a deserter whom you're bringing in."

"I don't see how you could have fallen asleep when your life depended on your staying awake," Dikar growled, but even though this was a dreadful thing Paine had done, his thoughts were not on it.

He was gaping at an enormous wall of rock that rose straight up from the edge of the River, gray rock so high that a lonely figure moving atop it seemed no bigger than Dikar's fingernail. The wall was like the Drop that circled the Mountain, but higher, and it went on and on along the River, as far as the eye could see.

"You've got the pass handy, Dikar," Paine said. "Haven't you?"

"Yes." Dikar touched the pocket in his green uniform where he'd put it. In doing this he turned so he saw the other side of the River. His breath caught in his throat.

THERE WAS some green along that edge of the River, but beyond the green—buildings. Not a few, as at West Point, but so many that they were like a forest of buildings, as many as the trees in the woods. The smallest was as high as the tallest tree in the Mountains.

But they could not be Buildings, piling higher and higher ahead there. They could not be anything men had made. Slender, graceful, they lifted to the sky, white in the pale dawn-light, and blue-gray, and dark-red as the leaves of autumn, and some touched with gold. High they soared till they were misty with height, till they were clouds piling in the sky, tipped with color by the sunrise; till they were like nothing Dikar had ever seen or ever dreamed of, a glory rooted not in the earth but in the heavens.

"What?" Dikar gasped, pointing. "What—?" and could say no more.

"The City," Paine answered. "New York." In that instant the risen sun flooded the City with golden fire, and there was one slim building that rose higher than the rest, an enormous finger pointing at God. The sunlight struck through it and Dikar saw that it was only a broken black tracery against the light.

The boat leaned over, was sweeping around in a long curve, driving straight for the shore. And Dikar saw now that there was scarcely a building whole in all the city, that some leaned crazily and some had great gaps bitten out of their sides. Here and there were spaces where there were no buildings at all.

Then the City was too near, too high, for Dikar to see it. He could only see that they had passed the green strip along the River, that they were shooting straight for a squat, ugly-looking building that stuck out into the greasy waters, a building that would have looked huge to him yesterday but now was small and dirty and mean.

Men were running out to the river-end of this building. Blacks in the green Asafric uniform, and they were carrying the long guns called rifles.

The boat bumped against the end of the building. The Blacks were lined along it, their rifles aiming at Dikar, their little red eyes cruel. An Asafric with only a revolver in his hand leaned over and said something Dikar could not understand.

Paine grabbed a rope that hung down and twisted it around an iron something that stuck up from the side of the boat. The Asafric yelled at Dikar. Dikar made sounds back up at him, a jabber that meant nothing to Dikar himself.

The Asafric looked mad. "Wat kind talk yoh big fella fool make? W'at kind brown-skin Black yoh be, make funny talk Ah no can un'stan?"

Dikar's heart skipped a beat. The Asafric had called him a

Black. "Good talk w'at ah make." He was getting away with it. "Talk mah people. Ah be Abyssin."

He put a foot up on the edge of the boat, reached to pull himself up to where the Asafric was. "Not so fas'," the latter grunted, jabbing his revolver almost in Dikar's face. "W'at name yoh come heah in boat? W'at name yoh hab dis white fella soldier along ob yoh?"

"W'at name it yoh business?" Dikar decided he might as well be fresh. "Tagloo no tell his business only to off'ser. Yoh bring off'ser, Tagloo tell him."

"All right, Sergeant Skoom! I'll take over." The voice was like a woman's. It belonged to the man with whose high-cheekboned, slant-eyed yellow face looked down at Dikar. "Here you! I am Lieutenant Sing Fong. What's all this?"

DIKAR SNAPPED his hand to his forehead, snapped it down again and stood straight, arms stiff at his sides the way Walt had told him to do when he talked to an officer. "Name ob me Tagloo, sah. Sebent' Foot Reg'ment, Fourt' Comp'ny." His borrowed uniform had on it a badge with those numbers.

"Dis white fella soldier desert f'om Wes' Point. He say he know how we can take fo't easy but he only tell Major Apgar, so my cap'n, Tsi Huan"—that was the name of Jubal's captain and it was signed to the pass Dikar was fumbling out of his pocket—"send me tak' him to de major, nobody else."

The officer took the pass, squinted at it. He made a little sound and kept looking at it. He was doing that for an awful long time. Dikar got all tight inside. The lieutenant's yellow, long-nailed hand strayed to the handle of his revolver. "Come up here. Both of you."

Dikar jumped up to the floor of the building, turned and helped Paine up, stood straight and stiff again, not letting his face show anything. The Black soldiers closed in around them. Sing Fong folded the pass—and stuck it into his own pocket.

"So you're to be taken to Major Apgar." Something, the little smile that played about his naked-looking mouth, the way he purred, maybe, reminded Dikar of a cat he'd seen, at West Point, playing with a bird it had caught and maimed. "No one less."

"Yaas, Lieut'nant." If Dikar jumped into the water— No. Fast as he could swim, the bullets from the Asafrics' rifles would be faster. "Dat be Cap'n Tsi Huan's ordeh."

"Just a minute, Lieutenant," Paine broke in, talking for the first time. "Let me tell you—" *Spat!* Sing Foo's fist lashed into Paine's mouth, so hard that he staggered backward, would have fallen if one of the Asafrics hadn't pounded a rifle butt into his back, straightening him up again.

"It seems to me," the officer remarked, casually, "that you American dogs should have learned by this time to speak to your masters only when you are spoken to. Straighten up. Stand at attention."

Captain Paine's eyes were those of a snake about to strike. "I think you will regret that," came from between his bloody lips, "when I have reported it to your superiors." He has courage, Dikar thought. He has more courage than I have.

Lieutenant Sing Foo's cat-smile deepened. "One more word from you," he murmured, and I will have your tongue torn out. Then he was barking: "Sergeant Skoom! Detail a guard of three privates and take these men to headquarters. You may use my car."

CHAPTER 6

HIS EXCELLENCY THE SPIDER

THE CAR was a little truck with high iron sides, painted green. A machine gun stuck out over its back. There were two seats. Paine was in the back one between two Black privates and Dikar was in the front between the other private and Sergeant Skoom, who was doing all the things that made the car start and stop and go the way he wanted it to go.

It went very fast along wide spaces between the buildings.

The buildings rose high above, so that it was as if they were at the bottom of deep ravines, very long and very straight with places on each side where people walked.

There were a lot of other cars going between the buildings, little ones like this and big trucks. These had only Asafrics in them but among the people walking there were many whites.

The whites were all stooped over and gray-faced, shambling, the women and children as well as the men. When an Asafric, yellow or black, came swaggering along, the whites made way for him even if they had to go out in the space where the trucks ran to do so. The Asafrics laughed a lot and talked very loudly, but the whites talked very low, if they talked at all, and they never laughed.

Some of the whites had the burned star on their brows and the eyes of these were empty as a dead man's. But that emptiness was better than what was in the eyes of the other whites.

This was fear. Men and women and children, the whites who lived in this city were afraid, and Dikar knew that they had been afraid so long that they had forgotten what it was not to be afraid, because he saw some of the things they feared.

Dikar saw a couple of white men carrying heavy bundles from a truck into a building. One of them stumbled and fell and the Asafric who was watching kicked him, and blood came out of his mouth. Dikar saw a bunch of Americans shuffling wearily along, chained together two by two, and the Asafrics who walked beside them had long whips that lashed out and cut rags and skin from their backs if they went too slowly.

The car passed a big flat space of ground covered by yellowing grass. Instead of trees, poles grew up out of the ground and each pole had a cross-piece sticking out from its top. From each cross-piece hung something that once had been a man but now was a bundle of rags and bones, swinging in the wind.

The smell in Dikar's nostrils was a smell of filth and rottenness, of sick bodies and sick minds; the City that from the River had looked so glorious was a place of desolation and despair.

Dikar tried to close his eyes, so that he would not see these things, but he could not keep them closed. He looked up high, so as not to see the people, and saw a building whose windows were smashed and blind, its insides gutted by fire. He saw another that was nothing but a black network of broken iron, rubble piled in the great hole above which it stood.

All of a sudden there was beside him a wall that went up and up so high that Dikar had to bend his head back as far as it would go to see the top. It was the unbelievable building that had seemed from the River to be a finger pointing at God.

The car slowed and stopped right in front of this great building, and Sergeant Skoom was telling Dikar and Paine to get out.

They obeyed.

SKOOM WALKED first, and then Paine and Dikar and behind them the three Asafric privates with their rifles ready to shoot. In this way they went into the building, into a room bigger than any Dikar had ever seen.

It was all stone, with a gold-painted roof and shining black walls, but all the stone was cracked and pieces were broken away everywhere so that the iron bones of the building showed through. And the room stank with the smell of Asafrics.

There were a great many Asafrics standing around, talking and laughing, but the room was so big they hardly seemed to be making any noise at all. An officer, a little man with a sharp, yellow face and shiny hair black as a crow's feathers, came toward them.

Skoom told them to stop and he went ahead to meet the officer, jerking his hand to his head and down again. He talked so low Dikar couldn't hear what he said, and the officer's narrow, slanted black eyes looked past Skoom at Dikar and Paine.

The way the officer looked at them made Dikar feel afraid.

The officer went to the wall and talked into a little box that hung on it. Then he came back to Skoom and said something;

Skoom's hand jerked up and down, and he came back to Dikar and Paine, his purplish, thick lips grinning.

"Yoh hab one big fella luck ob de debbil," he said to Dikar. "Yoh go see Viceroy Hashamoto hese'f."

"Hashamoto!" Dikar felt the strength go out of his body. He licked his lips, managed to say, "I no go see Viceroy. Cap'n Tsi Huan say I take white fella deserter to Major Apgar, nobody else."

"Dat all right." Skoom grinned. "You go see major too. He wid Viceroy w'en Lieutenant Sing Foo telefoam 'bout yoh, an' dey gib order bring yoh to Viceroy's quahtehs."

"But my white fella pris'ner say he not talk only to major," Dikar persisted. "He say—"

"That's all right, Tagloo," Paine broke in. "I'd rather the Viceroy heard what I have to say. Much rather."

"Come 'long," the sergeant said. "Ah no care w'at you radder or not radder. Come 'long befoh ah make yoh."

They started moving again, and Dikar felt a little better because Paine had said it was all right. Just what Paine was going to do, Dikar couldn't think, but he was very smart and must have worked out something to do.

They went through a door. It closed behind them. The space they were in wasn't much bigger than just enough to hold the six of them and another Asafric who was already in it. All of a sudden Dikar felt very heavy, his feet pressing hard down on the floor.

The hissing sound was sudden and frightening. But the snake noise stopped before he could get the knife out, and the door was opening again.

Sergeant Skoom must have made a mistake, Dikar decided, must have led them into the wrong place and now he was taking them to the right one. They went out again, but this was not the big room. It was a very narrow, long space, its roof white and much lower, doors all along both sides of it. Way down at the end there was a window and Dikar could see the sky through it.

In the short time they had been in the little room, everything outside it had changed.

Dikar's skin was tight and he was shivering. This was a more fearful magic than the electricity. For the first time he wasn't sure the Americans could lick the Asafrics. If they could do things like this....

SERGEANT SKOOM had stopped in front of a wide door at the end of the narrow space and was knocking on it. A muffled voice came through, and Skoom said something in his own language. The sergeant took hold of the handle on the door and pulled it open. The others went through it, and stopped short, and Skoom closed the door behind them.

Sergeant Skoom stood very straight and stiff, jerking his hand to his head, and the privates were frozen figures. There was a kind of greenish color under the Blacks' skin, and their eyes were scared. They were in a room three times as big as Headquarters at West Point. There were a lot of tables and chairs and benches in the room, all of different shapes and bright-colored, and the floor was bright-colored.

The same voice, no longer muffled, said something again. It came from a man who sat at a table far at the other end of the room, a little white man dressed in the green uniform of the Asafrics, his face pinched together like the shell of a nut, his nose hooked like an eagle's beak, his eyes very sharp and bright.

"Major Apgar say yoh two come." Skoom pushed Dikar and Paine, started them walking across the floor.

Another man sat behind the table toward which they walked. He was shorter even than Major Apgar, but he was almost as wide across as he was tall. His yellow face was round, and his eyes were drowned in the flabby bulge of his cheeks. His nose was bashed flat. He had no eyelashes nor eyebrows, and there was no hair on his face, on his great round head or on his soft-looking, swollen body that was covered only by thin, bright red cloth that gaped open down the front.

He was like a spider hiding under a leaf to which one string of its web was fastened, a spider bloated with the flies it has eaten.

Major Apgar was watching Dikar and Paine come across the floor, but Yee Hashamoto, Asafric Viceroy of America, was looking at the maps that strewed the table. He had a very small red mouth in his great, yellow moon of a face.

Dikar reached the nearer side of the table and stopped short, his hand going up to his head and down as Paine stopped alongside of him. Hashamoto's head lifted and his eyes looked at Dikar, and Dikar knew how a fly must feel, caught in a web and seeing the spider eye him from under the leaf. To escape that feeling he looked past Hashamoto at the wall behind him.

There was a door in that wall and it was a little open. Dikar's nostrils flared. From that door a smell came to him—a strange one to be in this place—the odor of flowers.

Major Apgar was talking to Dikar, his voice as cold as the winter streams on the Mountain.

He was talking in the language of the Asafrics. "Ah no can un'stan w'at de major talk," Dikar said. "'Cause ah be Abyssin—" He checked at the look on Apgar's face, and knew before the next words came from those thin lips what they would be.

"But it was in the Abyssinian dialect that I spoke," Major Apgar said, and there was a sudden gasp from Hashamoto. "I recognized that you were— You're *not!*" The major was up out of his seat, his pupils widening. "What are you? What—?"

"I'll tell you." This was Paine, and Dikar swung around to him in surprise. "This man is no more an Abyssinian than I am. He is an American spy."

He's given me away, thought Dikar, because I can't be saved, but that will save him and give him a chance to talk to Apgar alone.

"An American." A little pink tongue licked Hashamoto's lips and he looked even more like a spider. "Ahhh—and you?"

"An American too, but a loyal subject of your Excellency. No, wait!" Paine's uplifted hand stopped what the Viceroy was about to say next. "Wait and listen. You've been wondering how the Americans' underground operatives have been finding out your most secret plans. I can tell you where they're getting them from, whom they're getting them from. His eyes went to Major Apgar. "It is—"

"No!" Dikar shouted. He sprang, and his hand clamped the betrayal in Paine's throat. "You'll not tell!"

His fingers squeezed; his other arm went across the small of Paine's back. There was a shout somewhere, and a thud of feet running toward him, but Dikar was shoving Paine's purpling face away from him, was bending the upper part of him back over his rigid arm, while the lower part of Paine was clamped against Dikar's straining body.

Shouts somewhere, and a click of rifle bolts, and Apgar yelling. "Don't shoot, you fools. You'll kill the Viceroy." But there was a grating of bone against the swelling muscles of Dikar's arm and a scream shrill and terrible, tore through Dikar's throttling fingers. Paine's back snapped across Dikar's arm, like a dead branch.

Dikar let the body drop and saw green uniforms, black faces, leaping at him, saw clubbed rifles flailing. He roared and sprang to meet them, but a rifle butt pounded into his chest, staggering him back, and another paralyzed his arm. Blows rained on Dikar; he was pounded to the floor.

Dikar rolled on the floor and with darkening sight he saw an iron-covered rifle butt driving down at his head.

CHAPTER 7
TO SAVE A TRAITOR

"NO!" CAME a high, thin cry. "Don't kill him." The rifle butt hung, strangely motionless, over Dikar's head, and in the dizzy dark there seemed to be a flutter of blue above him. A woman's voice cried again, "Don't kill him," and the smell of flowers was very strong in his nostrils. The darkness welled up into Dikar's head and he went down, down into dark depths of pain.

Dikar swung up out of the dark and somewhere above him Hashamoto was saying, "You were right, Lisa. You were very right to stop these fools from killing him. He must know the traitor's name, and he will tell me. Oh, yes."

The darkness faded out of Dikar's eyes. He could see Sergeant Skoom leering down at him, little eyes redder than before, and the other Blacks, rifles clubbed and ready to beat Dikar down if he moved. He could see the gold braid on Benjamin Apgar's green uniform and a gross leg that must be Hashamoto's because it was covered with scarlet cloth.

"Of course I was right." The woman's voice was throaty now. "If I hadn't been coming to see what was keeping you and started to open that door just in time to hear what the other American said, this spy would be dead now and the rebels would keep on learning our secrets."

She hadn't just started to open that door, Dikar thought. It had been open all the time. She'd been listening. His head rolled, and he saw her, a soft blue robe fluttering about her slender, deep-breasted white body, her hair a cloud of yellow sunshine about her delicate features. With the movement pain reached deep into Dikar, wrenched a groan from his throat.

"He's coming to," Hashamoto said. "Put irons on him, Sergeant. Quickly."

Skoom knelt, grabbed Dikar's arms. Agony rushed through him, and he went down again into the darkness.

When he could see again he was slumped in a chair, iron cuffs on his wrists, on his ankles. Skoom was standing stiff in front of Hashamoto and the Viceroy was talking. "You will say nothing of this to anyone, nor will your men. Understand?"

"Yaas, Excellency. Ah understand."

"You had better." Very cruel was that round, yellow face. "If the traitor is warned and escapes, I shall know just whom to blame and that will be unpleasant for you. You may retire now to the corridor outside this room and wait there for further orders."

Skoom saluted, turned sharply away and marched out of the room, the other Blacks following. The three, Hashamoto and Apgar and Lisa, watched them go, none speaking until the door closed behind them.

"Now," Hashamoto murmured. "Now we shall ask our friend a question or two." He came toward Dikar and a humming sound came with him. The humming sound was caused by something in his pudgy hand. It was a very thin stick as long as Dikar's arm, and it shone in the light like the blade of a knife and quivered because it was so thin. The quivering was what made the humming sound.

Benjamin Apgar watched the scarlet-clothed, bloated form as it padded softly toward Dikar, and Apgar's wrinkled face was expressionless except for the eyes; they had the look of someone who was drowning and did not know how to save himself. And in Lisa's violet eyes there was, strangely, that very same look.

Yee Hashamoto stopped, three paces from Dikar's chair. "Stand up," he commanded, low-toned. "Get up on your feet."

DIKAR'S JAW set in a stubborn line. Then his face relaxed: He had thought of something: These iron cuffs on his wrists could crack a skull. He heaved, every muscle a separate agony, twisted, and was up out of the chair—

The thin stick whined, flashed down in front of Dikar. He

dodged back, almost fell, managed to keep his feet. The stick hadn't touched him.

The jacket of his uniform hung loose. The buttons from it were rolling across the floor.

Wheen! Dikar didn't even see the stick move that time, but he felt chill on his back. Green cloth fell down between his legs. *Wheen! Wheen!* Two slashes! He was naked above his waist except for the sleeves on his arms and two rags that hung from his shoulders. The thin stick had stripped him, but had never touched his skin.

"I have not lost my skill with this," Yee Hashamoto murmured, stroking it between the fingers of his free hand. "A sweet toy." Its humming was the noise a wasp made flying in the summer sun. "I can slice an inch of flesh from your body." Spittle was bubbling at the corners of his tiny, red mouth. "And another inch and another, stripping your skeleton clean while you live inside of it. I can deal the Death of the Thousand Cuts, which takes so very long to kill."

The floor heaved up and down beneath Dikar. If only the yellow spider would come nearer. No use to spring at him. That gray-white stick would meet one, would slash across one's eyes.

"But there will be no need for me to prove my skill," Hashamoto murmured. "I am quite sure that you are going to tell me the name of the traitor on my staff."

Dikar looked at him. Queer. The room was spinning.

"Are you not?" The stick rose, humming. "Answer me."

"No." Was this hoarse croak his voice? "No, I am not," Dikar croaked and sprang at the Viceroy, his manacled arms lifting. But he thudded to the floor, tripped by the irons on his ankles. He thrust fists against the floor, and was too weak to lift himself.

Fire burned across his back—the lash of the humming stick. A foot thudded into Dikar's side, turned him over, and he was staring up at an expressionless moon-face.

The thin stick hummed, hanging above Dikar, and there was a red smear on its shine and it dripped red drops. "Who is he?"

Yee Hashamoto murmured, his face expressionless. "What is his name?"

All the pain in Dikar's body seemed to drain into that one place where the stick had touched him. If Apgar tried to stop this he would only give himself away, and he must not do that. He had helped the Cause, he would help it again.

"You can kill me, but I won't tell you."

"I shall kill you, but not before you tell me." The stick hummed, lifting.

"Yee." It was Lisa's blue robe Dikar saw above him now, and Lisa was saying, "It's going to take a long time to make him speak, Yee." Her slender, white hand was on Yee Hashamoto's fat arm. "And once more you won't have time to take me flying. Turn him over to Ben Apgar."

The yellow man brushed Lisa's hand from his arm. "This man knows the traitor's name; I want that name. You understand, Lisa? This is no time for pleasure flying."

"You promised me, Yee. You gave me your word that nothing would keep you from doing it today."

"Then I break my promise."

"Again!" There was sharpness in Lisa's voice, sudden violent fire in her eyes. "This is the fifth time. Remember what *I* promised *you* yesterday when the report of trouble in the South and West came in and you said you couldn't go."

He was looking at her strangely. "What?"

"THAT IF we didn't go today, I was through. Go ahead with what you want to do." She was walking away, her blue robe whispering about her slenderness, "Take as much time as you want."

She reached the door through which she had come in, faced around, one hand on the door handle, the other at her throat. "Take all day, all week to do what Ben Apgar could do as well as you. Better perhaps." The skin at her throat was as white as the down on a pigeon's breast and looked as soft, as warm to the touch. "But don't come looking for me when you're done, because I won't be here."

"Lisa." Hashamoto's creased neck swelled with his anger. "You talk like that to me? You dare? There is still a whipping post, Lisa. I can still send you back to it. I can still have you flogged to the death from which I saved you."

"Of course you can." She smiled thinly. "And the whole army will laugh at you." But Dikar saw the flutter in her throat that told how terrified she was. "The whole army will laugh, whispering how even a white slave-woman preferred death on the whipping post to the attentions of the Viceroy.

"No, my dear. Whether you have me publicly flogged to death or privately murdered, the secret will leak out, and if you let me live, I will tell it. All your officers will be greatly entertained. When you give them an order they will salute, and turn from you and snicker, thinking of how a helpless woman despised you. Where will your discipline be then? Where will be your face?"

There was a choking sound in Hashamoto's throat.

"And when, on the other side of the world," Lisa went on, mercilessly, "your Emperor hears the echo of your army's laughter— One minute, my dear Yee. I give you one minute to come to me," Lisa said, and was gone.

After the door closed, there was only the hum of Hashamoto's thin stick and sound of his heavy breathing. Then Benjamin Apgar began to speak, low-voiced.

"The little devil. But she'll do it, Excellency. Nothing in God's world can keep her from doing it."

"Nothing—" Yee Hashamoto, Viceroy of all America, was a fumbling fat man. He spread his hands wide, said, "It was once said: 'It is safer to put your honor in keeping of man who hates you than in hands of woman who love—' Can I trust you, Benjamin Apgar?"

"In all the years, your Excellency, that I have served you, have you ever found reason to distrust me?"

"No." Hashamoto held out his stick, and queerly, it did not hum. "When I return, Major Apgar, I shall expect to hear the name of the traitor."

"You may expect it," Apgar answered, taking the stick, and Hashamoto was going across the room and out of the door.

"Poor Lisa," Apgar sighed. "She did not have the courage to die to save her own soul, but when it was her country—"

Trying to get up, Dikar saw the crumpled, shapeless thing that he had made of Captain Paine, and suddenly a lot of things were clear to him. Paine was the spy, not Morgan. Paine, not Morgan had slipped up behind Gary, dubbed him. It was Morgan who'd seen that murder, and Paine had shot Morgan.

The revolvers—if they had stopped to think about how they lay, the bloody, hair-matted one near Paine, the other so much farther away.

The plan to kill Walt and Dikar, to steal the boat and come down the River to tell, the Asafrics about Apgar—no wonder Paine had figured it out so quickly. He hadn't had to figure it out; it had been his own plan. He hadn't fallen asleep over the wheel at all. If Lieutenant Sing Fong had let him talk....

"But Lisa only postponed the inevitable," Apgar was saying. Dikar looked at him. "She will have to let Hashamoto come back some time, and then—"

The major's thin hand, like a bird's talons, held a revolver and it was pointing down at Dikar. "I'm sorry, son." The nutlike face had a queer smile on it. "But this is the most Lisa has gained for us—a bullet in your brain, another in mine."

CHAPTER 8

NO TYRANT RULES THE SKY

ODDLY, DIKAR was not afraid. "Wait," he said. "Listen. To make sure that he does not make me tell your secret, you must shoot me, of course; but you must not shoot yourself. You're needed, Major Apgar. America needs you now more than it ever did."

"Needs me?" The revolver wavered, ever so little. "No, son. I can do no more for America, now that I am no longer in touch with the Secret Net. I can do no more, and I have lived in hell too long, and I'm tired." It was almost as if he were pleading with Dikar for the right to die. "I have earned my rest."

"There can be no rest for anyone till America is free again." Dikar rocked up to squat on his haunches and the room started to circle again, the floor to heave, but at length the blur cleared. "I came here to tell you what you can do. What you must do. That is why I came looking for you."

"For me—yes. Yes, of course. I'd forgotten." Apgar pulled across his brow the edge of the hand that held the gun. "The lieutenant did report that you insisted on seeing me, and Hashamoto thought that so strange he had you brought up here. You have a message for me?"

"I have. From the President of the United States."

"The President!" Apgar looked startled. "He's escaped! But even if he has, what good? I saw him only last week, a dirt-crusted, bedraggled thing climbing the bars of his cage and eternally singing the *Star-Spangled Banner* in a shrill, cracked voice."

"The man you saw was the president of a dead America. The man who sent me to you is the Leader of a new America, an America that is only just now being born. Listen, Major Apgar." In a voice hoarse with pain Dikar told about Normanfenton and the Second Continental Congress, and a light began to come into Benjamin Apgar's face, and he was a tired old man no longer. Then Dikar told of the plan the Congress had made and Apgar turned quickly to the table, snatched up one of the maps Hashamoto had been studying.

"Here's the very place," he cried, smacking his hand on it. "The munitions depot at Dover, New Jersey, only eighty miles from West Point. You say you have captured plenty of trucks when you took the fort? With those we can make it there and back in one night.

"There's a well-paved highway between that isn't too well guarded, and Dover's garrisoned by only two companies. Blow up the explosives stored there and Hashamoto will be so enraged that he will forget all about his careful plans. Look here."

Apgar gathered the other maps in both hands. "The Viceroy has decided merely to keep watch on West Point while he dispatches bombing planes and troops to put down the insurrections in— But what's the use?" The excitement was abruptly out of him. "We can't get word to Fenton about all this. There's no way."

"There is," Dikar broke in. "There must be. Think, Apgar. Till the Viceroy gets back you're still a major on his staff. You still can give orders that will be obeyed by every Asafric. There must be some way."

"Wait! Maybe— Lie down there. Lie down and groan, and pretend to be just on the point of fainting." Apgar was stuffing the maps into an inside pocket of his coat as Dikar obeyed. "And pray that this will work. It will be a miracle if it does, but miracles sometimes happen."

Then he was calling in a loud voice, "Skoom! Sergeant Skoom!"

The wide door at the other end of the room opened. "Heah, sah."

"Bring your men in here," Apgar snapped. "On the double-quick, and make sure that door's locked behind you."

THEY CAME in, their feet thudding on the floor, their rifles jangling. "Line them up at attention," Apgar snapped. Skoom barked orders and the three privates were standing in a straight line across the floor before the major, with Skoom a step or two in front of them.

Dikar moaned, scrabbling the floor with his fingers. This was not all pretense of suffering, for every movement brought him agony.

Above him, Major Apgar was talking to the Blacks in their own language. Dikar could not understand, of course, but he learned afterward that this was what Apgar was saying: "You heard enough, before you were sent out of here, to know that someone has been betraying us to the American dogs, and that this carrion whimpering at my feet knows who the traitor is.

"He has been persuaded to tell us the name, but the man is so highly placed that the lightning of the Viceroy's wrath cannot strike him like a bolt from the skies. The Emperor's permission must be obtained before so much as a hand may be laid upon him.

"General Yee Hashamoto has gone to arrange for this, but meantime there is danger that the traitor may learn that he is discovered, and flee. It is needful, therefore, that this pig of a spy be hidden from knowledge of all till the Viceroy is ready to act swiftly. This is the task Yee Hashamoto has laid upon me, and upon you.

"The words you hear now come from my mouth but the voice is the voice of your Viceroy. The orders you hear are to be obeyed no matter who gives you contrary orders, unless it be the Viceroy himself, by my mouth or by his own. Is that understood?"

"It is understood, sah," Skoom answered. "We understand and obey."

"Very well. We are flying the prisoner to a camp in the northern woods where we will guard him till the traitor is safely in jail. Skoom! Unlock those irons from the prisoner's feet but leave those on his wrist.

"You, on the end there! You are of a size with him. Remove

your tunic and clothe him in it. You will lock the outer door when we depart and remain here, opening to no one until the Viceroy relieves you. You other two will come with us and you will shoot down anyone, officer or enlisted man, who attempts to speak with the prisoner, or to hinder us."

CURIOUS EYES followed them as they walked out through the enormous stone-walled room. But the Asafrics quickly saluted when they saw the forbidding frown on Major Apgar's face; they did not attempt to speak to the Blacks or to their iron-cuffed prisoner.

Outside, Dikar was ordered into the back seat of the car between the two privates. Apgar sat in front with Skoom.

The car started off. Apgar leaned over and spoke to Skoom. Skoom grinned and touched something on the wheel he gripped. Dikar jumped as a siren started to howl and looked up into the sky for planes; then he realized that the howling came from the front of the car, and that the car was going faster.

The other cars and trucks were scattering from in front of them, like minnows when a trout darts at them from beneath a shadowy rock; and they were going so fast that there were tears in Dikar's eyes and he could see only a gray blur of buildings speeding past.

Then, suddenly, there were no buildings, but blue sky and a wide, white road and a white lattice of iron rising into the sky, with water far beneath. A few moments later the car was running across an enormous flat field, and it was slowing, the siren moaning to silence.

Across that field, as far as Dikar could see, stretched lines and lines of planes, huge planes shining silvery in the sunlight and medium-sized ones red as the breast of a tanager and little ones black as crows. And buzzing like bees about the planes were hundreds of Asafrics.

The car rocked to a stop near a line of the small black planes. Major Apgar sprang to the ground. A yellow-faced officer came running and stiffened to attention.

"I want one of your fastest pursuit planes," the major snapped. "One that is ready to take-off at once."

Slant eyes glanced at Dikar, shifted back to Apgar. "The major has a flight order from the field-commandant, of course."

"I have not. But I have a verbal order from the Viceroy, and I'm in a hurry."

"But Major Apgar"—the officer looked puzzled—"the Viceroy—"

"Are you questioning an officer of the Viceroy's personal staff? Do you dare?"

The lieutenant paled. "No, sir. By no means, sir."

"Then give me a plane and be quick about it."

"Yes, sir." The officer wheeled about, pointed to one, at the end of the nearest line. "That is my own and I know she is one of our fastest." A number of Asafrics were swarming over it. "We are just finishing the morning checkup on her, and—"

"Get those men out of her and turn her over to me. Quickly."

"Yes, sir." The officer started away. Major Apgar turned to the car, said, "All right, Skoom, get them out of there." Skoom jabbered to the privates and they grabbed Dikar's arms, hauled him out to the ground. Then they were all hurrying toward the little black plane.

A WHISTLE shrilled somewhere, loud, ear-piercing. All over the field Asafrics were stopping what they were doing, were looking upward. Dikar's little group reached the plane where the last Asafric was tightening something on a wing, and the lieutenant was saying to Major Apgar, "I must tell you that we've just received warning that a line squall is coming down from the north. All but absolutely necessary flights have been called off."

"Damn the squall," Apgar growled. He glanced up into the sky and Dikar saw a tiny muscle twitch at the corner of his cheekbone. "I'm not calling this one off." Dikar looked up too and saw a plane, bright green as leaf-buds in the spring, coming down on a long, swift slant. "Here. Give me your goggles."

"Yes, sir." The officer handed something to the major. "But I shall need them, flying you—"

"You're not flying us. There will be no room for you. Skoom!" Apgar whirled to the sergeant. "Get everyone into the plane. Snap to it."

Skoom was jabbering to the privates He was pointing to the green plane which had landed now and was running along the ground, straight toward them. "Skoom!" The major snapped: "Do you hear me? Get the prisoner into the plane."

The sergeant said something, started toward him. The green plane had stopped, about a hundred yards away. The Asafric workmen were carrying a set of short steps to it, placing the steps against it, just under a door in its side. The door was opening.

Apgar's voice was sharp, angry, behind Dikar—the sergeant's answer sullen-sounding. The privates' fingers were tightening on Dikar's arms. The door of the green plane opened, and a figure in glittering uniform stepped into the sunlight—a bloated figure with a round, moon face. Yee Hashamoto!

The sudden roar of an engine drowned out the voices behind Dikar. The Viceroy glanced that way.

Dikar saw Hashamoto's tiny mouth open, saw his fat arm lift to point at them. The Asafrics were turning, were starting to run toward Dikar and the black plane. Hashamoto jumped down off the steps and came on, yelling.

"He's seen us," Dikar cried. "He knows who we are." The Major was in the black plane, and Dikar shouted at him: "Get away. Leave me and get away."

Skoom had hold of Dikar's arm with one hand and was pulling a revolver from his belt with the other. But Dikar's sudden leap tore him from the Black's grasp. He lifted his arms, clamped together by the cuffs, brought them down. The manacles struck Skoom's head savagely. The sergeant was falling and Dikar was leaping over his fallen body, and Apgar was dragging Dikar over the side of the plane.

The plane was moving, but shots were barking all around, and Dikar could hear Hashamoto's bellow above the engine's roar. Dikar dragged himself upright and saw the soldiers closing in on the plane, the little guns in their hands spitting fire. Right ahead Dikar saw the green plane; a flutter of blue appeared in its open door, and a delicate face framed by hair like yellow sunshine.

But the black plane was sluggish to rise. It drove forward, only a few feet above the ground, and there directly in its path was the green plane, terrifyingly near. Then Dikar saw the ground drop suddenly away and in that same instant a rending crash threw him violently to one side. Another shock and he was being whirled somewhere between the earth and the sky.

IT SEEMED an endless time before Dikar was no longer being wrenched about, but at last he was carried steadily, and the shot-sounds, the shouting, seemed far away under him. He dragged himself up, somehow, till he could look over the plane side. He saw sky, looked down and saw the field skimming away. The little men down there were running about like ants.

"The miracle!" he heard Benjamin Apgar yell. "The miracle has happened. Our landing gear's torn away but we're still in the air, and we've got a chance now to get away."

Wind whipped Dikar's face, but still he stared down at the field. He could see a heap of broken green and a spot of blue near it that was very still.

"She did as best she could what she was best fitted for," Dikar whispered to himself, "an at Evenin' Council the Boss of us all will say to her, 'Well done, Lisa.'" Then he felt a quick impact of terror that left him weak.

He'd realized suddenly that he was in the air, high in the air, and that there was nothing to hold him there, nothing but this shivering, frail thing they called a plane.

Dikar's legs buckled under him and he fell to the plane's

floor, groveling. He'd been scared before but never like this. Never like this.

"The storm warning must have turned Hashamoto back." Apgar's voice came to him, from far away, it seemed. "And he landed just at the wrong time for us, but we got away in spite of— Oh! Maybe we haven't got away yet. Look!"

The sky was filled with sound, with a rumble of thunder. Dikar's face, his palms, his whole body, were wet with cold sweat, but this seemed to have somewhat purged him of his terror. He had strength again to lift his head and look back the way Apgar had pointed.

Far back, far below, the field had shrunk so small that Dikar's hand might almost cover it, but black specks were streaking up from it, rising swiftly into the fathomless blue of the sky, and Dikar knew that these were the planes of the Asafrics pursuing them.

"Can they catch us?" Dikar demanded, turning to the weazened little man who crouched in the front of the plane, his hands clutching a stick stuck up from its floor. "Can you get us away from them?"

"I don't know," the answer came through the roaring in the sky. "But I'm going to make a damned good try."

CHAPTER 9

THUNDER IS A FRIEND

FAR AHEAD gray-black clouds piled up in the sky, the clouds of the storm that had turned Yee Hashamoto back, but about them the sky was clear as the water of a Mountain stream, as crisply cold.

Beneath, fold on fold, the hills that had crouched blackly ominous in the night were patterned with squares of green, darker and lighter, and yellow. Fine white lines that were broad roads meandered among them and from the bottom of a long crease in the hills glinted silvery-blue a ribbon no wider than Dikar's arm. The great River.

"Can you fight with a machine gun, Dikar?"

"I never have," Dikar answered Major Benjamin Apgar's question, looking at the red marks where the iron cuffs had ribbed the skin from his wrists. The cuffs were gone because, luckily, Apgar had taken from Skoom the key to them before they left headquarters. "But I can try, if I have to."

"Well, you're going to have to, all right. Look back."

Dikar obeyed. The black specks hung in the blue, far back, just as they had hung since they'd started out. No! One was a little larger, a little nearer the others. It was growing, very slowly, but still growing so that already Dikar could make out its spread wings, the blurred circle at its head that gave it strength to fly.

"This is one of their fastest pursuits," Apgar said grimly. "But that one is faster. It's going to catch us long before we reach West Point."

"What do we do then?" Dikar asked, quietly.

"We fight. See that machine gun behind you? Sit down on the floor beside it. There is a little tube, just at the level of your head. Close one eye and look through with the other."

Obeying, Dikar gasped. The leading Asafric plane had jumped forward miles, was almost on top of them. He jerked his head away. No. It was still back there, only a little nearer than it had been before.

"That's the sight," Apgar was saying. "You see those crossed hair lines? Where they join, the bullets will hit on your mark. The handle under the near end of the gun will move it."

He went on, telling Dikar how to aim the machine gun, how to load it, how to fire it, and by the time he had finished the pursuing plane was as near, almost, as it had seemed when Dikar first looked through the sight.

Bluish lines streaked the sky; there was a loud *rrrrt, rrrrrt.* There was a bright spot on the wing beside Dikar. Others! The

Asafric plane was roaring at him. The *rrrttt* was behind Dikar, nearer.

He turned. It was coming from the machine gun in front of Apgar, and beyond, between their own plane and the up-slanting hills, was the Asafric plane. Black-goggled men crouched in it. The hills and the plane swung up, over, down again in front of Dikar. He caught the Asafric plane on the crosshairs of his sight, pressed the trigger; he heard and felt the machine gun's harsh sound, and then the plane and the hills were gone....

SUDDENLY THE Asafric plane was whirling away, spinning crazily and dropping, flames bursting from it, and the plane he was in was tossing frantically no longer. Apgar was calling back, "All right, Dikar? Are you all right?"

"Yes," Dikar gasped, not quite sure, for there was fire across his one shoulder and there was sticky wetness on his forehead when he lifted his hand to it. "I think so." Turning, he saw that one arm of Apgar's hung limp by his side, its sleeve darkening. "But you're hurt!"

"No," Apgar said. "Not bad." The light within his face was even brighter; his eyes were shining. "I've not forgotten," he cried. "It's been years but I haven't forgotten how to handle a plane in a dog-fight."

"A dog-fight? I didn't see any dogs."

Apgar laughed and for an instant Dikar thought he heard one of the Boys of the Bunch laugh, so young and joyous was the sound. But then Dikar saw that the sky was all black-gray, close ahead, saw lightning streak the high-piled clouds.

"The storm!" he cried. "We're flyin' right into it!" And the sky was filled with thunder, but the thunder was from behind. Dikar wheeled, saw that the planes of the Asafrics, those that were left, were much nearer and coming fast. "The planes, Apgar! The other planes. We're going slower, and they're catching us!"

"The fight held us up and crippled us," Apgar's answer was blown back to Dikar on the wind. "The storm waits ahead,

Dikar, and the death lies behind. But be damned to them both, for between them, see is West Point."

Dikar looked down and saw the gray buildings of West Point nested very small in the encircling hills. A great shout of joy rose in his throat.

A white cloud puffed, just below the plane, and another little white cloud; the plane rocked and straightened, and rocked again, and sharp thunder struck at Dikar.

"They're shooting at us." Apgar pounded the stick with his good fist "In West Point they're shooting at us with their Archies. We can't get down in the face of their fire."

Thunder rolled in the storm ahead, and thunder rolled from the planes coming behind, and sharp thunder struck at Dikar from the little white puffs beneath.

"They think we're leading a squadron of Asafrics to attack them, Dikar: They think we're the enemy. After all we've gone through, to be killed at last by our friends— We have no way to let them know who we are."

"Yes we have," Dikar cried. He was tearing off his green uniform, coat, trousers. "We have one way." He was naked as when he roamed the Mountain. "Circle, Apgar! Circle above that flag down there."

"What—what are you going to do, Dikar?"

"I know they have tubes there by the Archies, through which they can see far and far. I'm going to let them see me, and they'll know who I am because I'm naked."

"But they can't see you, here in the cockpit, from below!"

"They'll see me where I'm going," Dikar flung back, and he was climbing up out of the place Apgar called the cockpit. He was climbing out on the wing torn by bullets, and the wind took hold of him.

THE WIND, stronger than any storm wind Dikar had ever known, fought to tear him from the wing. Thunder rolled from the storm clouds, from the black planes, from the Archies below;

and the thunder tossed the plane, shaking it, trying to shake Dikar from its wing, to cast him down and down till he smashed on the Plain below, between the gray buildings of West Point.

But Dikar clung to wires with both hands and would not let the wind tear him from the wing, would not let the Archies shake him from it, Dikar leaned far out, and below him the flag whipped in the storm wind, red and white and blue. Dikar let go with one hand, his feet clinging to the very edge of the plane, and leaned far out and waved his free hand to the little men on the roofs from which the Archies barked their thunder.

And suddenly the plane was not tossing any longer in the thunder of the Archies, and a faint sound of cheering came up to Dikar from below. The white puffs of the Archies were bursting far behind now, were bursting about the black, pursuing planes. The pursuing planes were lifting above the reach of the Archies, but Dikar's plane was sliding down the breast of the wind to the Plain that was hemmed in by the gray buildings of West Point.

Somehow Dikar tumbled back into the cockpit. Thunder clapped, deafening, but it was only the thunder of the storm. "Great stuff, son," he heard Apgar exclaim, and then Apgar groaned. "We have no landing gear."

"No landin—" Dikar gasped. "What does that mean?"

"It means that I've got to take her in on her belly. Miracle! We'll need a dozen miracles to live through this. Hold tight!"

There was only sound, vast sound blotting out all else. And then silence, darkness—light in the darkness, little yellow tongues of fire, licking toward Dikar.

Dikar could not move, could not get away from the fire. Something was holding him.

Thunder! A clap of thunder that burst the sky. Then a hissing like a thousand snakes—the hissing sound of rain. The air solid with rain that beat down on Dikar, that beat down and drowned the flames.

Wet hands were dragging Dikar out of the wreck of the

plane. Dimly he saw faces in the rain—Walt's, Normanfenton's. He saw vague figures gathered about a limp form, carrying it. The rain-curtain parted. The form was Benjamin Apgar's, and his eyes were open, and he was smiling. He was not dead. Benjamin Apgar was alive, and the plans, the maps, were safe.

"Dikar!" Marilee's voice was crying his name. "Oh, Dikar." Marilee was sobbing his name. Marilee's arms were around him, her lips were on his, and his head was on Marilee's breast.

It was sweet to sleep with his head pillowed on Marilee's soft breast.

DIKAR AWOKE. He was on his bed in the little House that was his and Marilee's, and night pressed black against the window. Out of the night came a thunder.

"The trucks, Dikar." Marilee was here by his bedside, gray eyes grave on his, smiling at him. "They're starting out for the raid on Dover."

"Starting!" Dikar pushed at the bed to get up, "I've got to—"

His hands were strangely clumsy; they were great white bundles, wrapped in cloth. The white stuff wound his body. Marilee's small hand pushed Dikar down on the bed. She was so strong suddenly—or was he so weak?

"You're not going anywhere, my dear," Marilee murmured. "You're staying here with me. You've done your job for today."

"For today. But tomorrow—"

"Tomorrow and tomorrow and tomorrow. There will be many tomorrows for us, Dikar, and each tomorrow will have its task for which you are fitted, and each task you will do well, because you are Dikar.

"But best of all there will be a new Tomorrow for America, a grand and shining Tomorrow for a free America, the long night of slavery ended, the sunrise come at last."

"Please, God," Dikar whispered. "Let there be sunrise, To-morrow."

LONG ROAD
TO TOMORROW

From: A History of the Asiatic-African World Hegemony, Zafir Uscudan, Ph.D (Bombay) LL.D (Singapore) F.I.H.S., etc. Third Edition, vol. 3, Chap. XXVII, pp 983 ff.

The night before the Asafrics captured New York, completing their conquest of the Western Hemisphere and thus of the entire Occidental World, an attempt was made to evacuate several thousand children from the doomed city.

The motorcade was discovered by a Yellow airman who, in the report discovered by the writer among the charred archives unearthed beneath the ruins of the Empire State Building, claimed to have entirely destroyed it by machine-gun fire and a few judicious bombs.

He was mistaken, however, in that one truck of the hundreds escaped. Among its load of children between the ages of four and eight was a youngster then known as Richard (or Dick) Carr, the very individual celebrated in legend as Dikar.

The aged couple who were the only adults with the group contrived somehow to bring the children unobserved to an uninhabited mountain deep within the forested recreation area that at the time stretched for some miles along the west bank of the Hudson. No more ideal sanctuary than this height could have been found.

Not only did thick woods screen its surface from aerial reconnaissance, but quarrying operations had ringed its base with a precipitous cliff so that the only practicable approach was by a

Silently Dikar led the Bunch up the cliffs to battle.

narrow viaduct of rock that the stoneworkers had left for their trucks.

Barely, however, had the party begun to orient itself when an Asafric platoon appeared on the plain below, with the evident intention of scouting the mountain. In this desperate emergency the two old people blew up the narrow ramp heretofore mentioned, burying under tons of riven boulders the green-uniformed soldiers—and themselves.

The children, afterward to be known as The Bunch, were now completely isolated from an inimical world. As to how they survived the primitive environment in which they found themselves we can only guess. Survive they did, for a dozen years later we find a band of youths bronzed, half-naked, and armed with only bows and arrows, descending on an Asafric motorized column to snatch from his chains the man called Norman Fenton.

THIS AMAZING foray is conceded to have been the first skirmish of the Great Uprising, but it was the capture of the Asafric stronghold at West Point, for which General Fenton's memoirs give full credit to Dikar and his Bunch, that set ablaze the fires of rebellion throughout a heretofore cowed American nation.

In preceding chapters we have seen how a ragtag and bobtail mob rallied around Norman Fenton at West Point, how the Second Continental Congress came into being here and elected Fenton President and Commander-in-Chief of the Armies of Liberation, how here was evolved the brilliant strategy with which Viceroy Yee Hashamoto found it so difficult to cope.

The reader doubtlessly recalls the essential elements of these tactics; the feinted raid on some sparsely garrisoned outpost, the real assault on the stronghold weakened by the dispatch of reinforcements to the point first threatened, the looting of the fortress of its guns, ammunition, all its portable munitions, the Americans' swift dispersal before the Asafric planes and tanks could return to annihilate them.

They split up into roving groups, well armed now and ferocious as only men can be who bear on their backs the scars of cruel whips, in their hearts the memory of homes in flames.

All across the continent these guerilla bands harassed Hashamoto's far-flung, thin lines. They ambushed and slew the small detachments through which he had maintained his subjection of his white slaves.

It is apparent how well Dikar and his brothers were fitted for such a campaign. Silent brown shadows never more than half-seen, they stalked men now instead of deer, and all the woodcraft they had learned on their Mountain, their tireless endurance, even their naive ignorance of fear, came to their aid in their new pursuit.

Is it any wonder that about the hidden campfires the tales of their prowess should grow to sagas of supernatural feats? Is it remarkable that it should be whispered that they were not flesh and blood at all but, risen out of long-forgotten graves, the same lean-flanked forest rangers who once seized Ticonderoga from the scarlet-garbed mercenaries of an earlier oppressor?

FROM THE writings of Walt Bennet, Fenton's devoted aide, we learn how tremendously the growing myth bolstered the patriots' morale, but it does not appear that during that first memorable winter the Bunch otherwise greatly influenced the course of the Uprising to which they had given its great Leader.

By the beginning of spring, the Asafrics, while still nominally in command of the entire country, had for all practical purposes been compelled to relinquish their hold on vast stretches of territory.

Save for the fortified strongholds to which they had retreated, they had virtually abandoned the great central plain north of the Panhandle of Texas, from the Rockies to the Missouri-Iowa-Minnesota border. East of the Mississippi they had fared somewhat better, but a map colored black where Hashamoto was still in full control would have shown two enormous patches of lighter hue.

The larger of these had spread northward from the Americans' first foothold at West Point to include virtually all New England, south to Georgia. New York City itself remained the Asafric Headquarters and a hundred-mile wide strip all along the seacoast lay under the shadow of their fleet's big guns. But the Americans commanded the central half of Pennsylvania, and Piedmont Virginia and the Carolinas to the western slope of the Blue Ridge Range.

On the other side of the Appalachians, Fenton's forces had retrieved the southern three-quarters of Indiana, Kentucky, and Tennessee as far east as the Cumberland River.

These latter two liberated regions approached each other most nearly in the neighborhood of the Great Smokies, and the strip separating them contained Norris Dam and other works at the head of the Tennessee Valley development.

If General Fenton could close this gap, not only would he cut in half the Asafric Army of the East, but he would be enabled to shut off the supply of electric energy to the industries of the deep South. This, in the last week of April, he moved to attempt.

But Viceroy Yee Hashamoto was fully aware of the strategic importance of this region, and he held the mile-high Smokies in force....

CHAPTER 1

WORLD OF THUNDER

SINCE THE day when the Asafric Planes first came into the sky over Wespoint, Dikar had heard their thunder many times. Many times he had heard the black eggs scream earthward out of the planes' opening bellies, heard the eggs burst in terrible sound.

But this was something even more terrible—a noise too great to hear. Dikar felt it rather, like an enormous hammer that never lifted but only got heavier and lighter and heavier again as it pounded him into the ground on which he lay face down.

The thunder was a hammer pounding him and a hammer somehow inside of him, pounding outward against the walls of his body till it seemed his body must burst like a bomb.

Outside him and inside him was the thunder and Dikar was a part of the thunder, the thunder a part of Dikar. Dikar was one with the thunder, one with its terror.

Yet one thought remained with him, in spite of the hammers beating his body and his brain—the thought that somewhere near him lay Marilee.

He had caught her up in his arms when the sky suddenly darkened with the black planes and he'd half-jumped, half-fallen into this gully. She had pulled from his arms to lie beside him as the thunder of the Asafric guns pounded down on them from the smoking tops of the mountains.

Was Marilee still here beside him? Or had some bit of flying iron, some sharp arrow of splintered wood, taken her from him forever?

Dikar got hands under his great chest. The muscles of his broad shoulders tightened. The muscles in his arms bulged. His arms quivered, straightened, lifted the weight on his shoulders. He raised his face from the red earth, and he looked to where Marilee should be.

Dikar saw nothing but green brush, green leaves, beaten down as no storm had ever beat down the brush on the Mountain. He stared, a huge fear rising in him; and then he gave a choked cry. For now he saw a white sarong that clung to the graceful young body of a Girl. He saw an arm, a shoulder, rounded, silken-skinned. In the hollow of a beloved throat he saw a pulse fluttering.

Some gust of sound brushed aside a spray of quivering leaves and Dikar saw the firm little chin, the delicate oval of Marilee's face.

WITHIN THE shadow of their long lashes, Marilee's gray eyes were big with terror. They saw Dikar and into them came a sudden smile.

A beam of sun was somehow in the thunder-shaking gully. It made little glints of red in the rippling cascade of brown and shining hair on which Marilee lay as on a bed. It made a shining in Dikar's blue eyes; and now the thunder that beat at Dikar was noise only, no longer terror.

Dikar smiled at Marilee, and he came up on his knees and looked over and past Marilee for the Boys and the Girls he had led so far from their Mountain.

The gully was narrow and its side steep, and it was filled by a tangle of bushes with long, thick leaves and great purple and white flowers like none Dikar had ever seen before. Peering into that thunder-tossed tangle, Dikar saw a little white bundle of fur, a long-eared rabbit crouched flat to the ground, its eyes glazed with terror. It crouched there right next to Franksmith, and did not fear him.

Franksmith's arm was flung out to one side and his hand clasped tight the hand of a black-haired Girl, Bessalton, Boss of the Girls. The sight of that brought a sudden warmth to Dikar's heart. Although most of the older Girls of the Bunch had found themselves mates, Bessalton had walked alone, since Tomball had died, and it was good that she would be alone no longer.

Past those two were more of the Bunch, flat to the ground, but even Dikar's sharp eyes could hardly make them out.

The Girls of the Bunch in their white sarongs were a little easier to see than the Boys who wore dappled fawn-skins that melted them into the shadows. All of them lay very still the way they'd fallen when they jumped into the gully, as still as the rabbit there by Franksmith.

The creatures of the woods lie very still when there is a danger too strong for them to fight and too swift for them to run from. This was a thing the Boys and the Girls had learned from the animals and the birds.

The gully was narrow and deep, and just as the leaf-roof of the Mountain's woods had hidden the Bunch from the Asafric planes, its thick brush tangle might hide them here. Dikar looked up to make sure that the green tangle was thick enough overhead—and his breath caught in his throat.

There was no hiding roof over him. The wind of the thunder had stripped the leaves and the great purple flowers from the branches of the brush and was stripping the very bark from the branches. Dikar could look right through what had been a safe covert. He could see clods of earth flying over the gully on the breast of the thunder-wind, and bits of wood that had been trees. And there were flying red fragments that could be human flesh.

NOT ONLY the Bunch had been caught here when the black planes came into the sky and the guns started to thunder from the mountain-tops. Hundreds of other Americans had moved down into this valley. From far away they had marched by night, slept by day, to gather here in answer to the orders General Normanfenton had sent out over the Secret Net.

Never before had so many Americans marched together. An Army, Dikar's friend Walt had called them. Never before had an army of Americans moved so far, so slowly, and this had worried Dikar, worried him all the more because till today the Asafrics had made not the least try to stop them.

Yesterday Walt had laughed when Dikar told him about his worry and begged him to tell Normanfenton to be careful.

"Hashamoto has no idea of what we're up to," Walt had said. "All the Shenandoah Valley down which we have come, and this northwest corner of North Carolina, was swept clear of his Blacks a month ago, and no white man or woman would betray us.

"We have one more night to march, my boy, and one more day to sleep. Tomorrow night, we'll surprise the Asafrics in their mountain stronghold while our friends in Tennessee storm the Cumberland Gap from the other. By sunrise, two days from now, the Smokies will be ours."

"The Smokies?" Dikar had repeated.

"Look." Walt had pointed, and Dikar had seen that what he'd thought a blue cloud low in the sky was really an up-tossing of the earth such as he'd never seen before. "Mountains," Walt had answered the question in Dikar's face, "so high that you could put your Mountain on top of one like itself, and another on top of those, and still not have them as high as the lowest of those. They're so high that there's always mist about their summits, and that's why the Indians called them the Smoking Mountains.

A shadow had darkened Walt's face. "General Fenton was telling me, only last night, how when he was very young he heard over the radio Franklin Roosevelt's speech dedicating a great National Park there, to the enjoyment and pleasure of our people for all time."

"For all time," he had repeated, bitterly, and then had said, "Up there is an Asafric army, Dikar, but its officers don't know we're anywhere within hundreds of miles of them."

He'd been so sure of that, it had been no use for Dikar to tell him about the tracks he'd seen in soft ground, of feet turned in at the toes the way the feet of the Blacks turn in. It had been no use for Dikar to tell him how the breeze had brought him, now and again in the past week, the smell of Blacks very near. Walt had been sure everything was all right, and Walt was lots smarter than Dikar. Hadn't Normanfenton picked Walt to be always close to him?

So the army had marched all last night. This morning, before the sun rose, they had found sleeping places in barns and houses, under bushes, in woods like this one where the Bunch had slept. Almost as good as the Bunch at hiding themselves were the other Americans. They had learned to be, this last winter.

But Dikar, lying by Marilee on a sweet-smelling bed of ferns, had not slept. Through the boughs of the tree over him he'd watched the sky grow pale with the coming dawn. He'd seen the red blush of sunrise touch the tops of the mountains, close now and so high his breath was taken away looking up and up. He'd seen the brightness spread up there.

And he had seen a black speck come into the sky from behind those mountain tops, and another, and another, while a distant low thunder of planes growled in his ears. Before he could cry out there had been a bright flash from the mountain top, and with that the first black egg had dropped screaming from the belly of the first black bird—

A burst of flame swept over Dikar's head, blinding him. The gully side heaved. Its green was cracked with earthy redness. It was all red earth and it was falling down upon him.

"*Marilee!*" Her name burst from his throat in a great shout he himself could not hear, and Dikar threw himself across his mate, just as the earth came down and buried them both.

CHAPTER 2

THE BOSS AND THE BUNCH

THE BLACKNESS was a solid thing against Dikar's down-bent face. On Dikar's back was a terrible weight of dark earth, so that his straddled thighs, his thrust-down, aching arms, shook.

Dikar's chest heaved, desperately pulling in dank air out of the black space that was roofed by his back, walled by his arms, his thighs and the earth crushing against his sides.

"Dikar!" From the black space out of which Dikar's failing strength still held the earth came Marilee's cry. "Dikar. Where are you?"

"Here." Hard to talk as to breathe. "Right above you. You— all right?"

"All right, Dikar. My legs—I can't move my legs but—but I think that's because of the dirt on 'em. Oh Dikar!" A sob caught at her voice. "What are we goin' to do?"

"Do?" How long could he hold up this awful weight on his back hold it from crushing Marilee? "Get out of this." But how was he to get Marilee out of this living grave?

"It's movin', Dikar! The dirt's comin' in over me!"

"Just settlin', Marilee. I'm holdin' it."

"If I could only see you, Dikar. If I could only feel your arms around me, only once more."

Only once more! She knew he'd lied. "I'm holdin' it," he lied again, because he could not think what else to say. The earth was alive with movement, alive with its blind will to crush them. Dikar could hear the soft, dreadful rub of the earth as it moved in under him.

Where it moved, Marilee was talking, but not to Dikar. "Now I lay me down to sleep." She was saying the Now-I-Lay-Me the Old Ones taught the Bunch to say each night when Bedtime came. "I pray the Lord my soul to keep. An' if I die before I wake—"

"No," Dikar groaned into the dark. "No, Marilee. You're not goin'—to die." But the terrible weight of earth was growing, it was pressing the strength out of his arms and back.

"Quick, Dikar! It's comin' over my face." It was sliding in under his belly. "Quick! Before—"

Marilee's voice choked off. Dikar's arms let him down. Dikar's arms found Marilee's warm body. Earth, following down, crushed Dikar's body to Marilee's. Somehow his lips found hers.

All of a sudden the thunder was loud in Dikar's ears again, and he could breathe! "Dikar!" a near voice jabbered. "Dikar, man!" Dikar's head flung back and he blinked earth from his eyes as the voice cried, "Dikar, old fellah." There was light in Dikar's eyes again and upside down, in the light was a hollow-cheeked, earth-smudged face he knew.

The face of Walt, his friend.

"Thank God!" Walt gasped, his hands scraping earth away from around Dikar. "Thank God you're alive! When I saw the bank cave in on you—"

Dikar heaved up and was on his knees, and his tight-clenched arms brought Marilee up out of the red earth. She clung to him, and he could feel her quick breathing.

WALT WAS still jabbering, and now there were hurrays around them. Dikar saw that it was Franksmith hurraying, and Bessalton and pimply-faced Carlberger. And there were others of the Bunch here too, and they were all red with earth, their hands red and shapeless with earth.

"It fell on us, too," Franksmith burst out. "But not deep, and when we shoved up out, we saw Walt here diggin' with his hands so we came an' helped him."

Dikar wondered that he could hear them all so plain in spite of the thunder and then it came to him that the thunder was much less loud than it had been before. He looked up into the sky. There were no planes in it now.

"Bomb loads don't last forever," Walt answered Dikar's look, "and they'll have to fly so far back to get more that they'll hardly be able to return before nightfall. But the guns are still at it."

Bessalton and Alicekane took Marilee from Dikar's arms and started to clean the earth from her. "Walt!" Dikar went cold all over with a sudden thought. "Why're you here? Is Norman-fenton—"

"The President's in a deep cave up ahead; I took him there." Walt's gray-blue uniform, from the stores they'd found at Wespoint, hung in rags about him. "What you said yesterday had me jittery." There was stiff hair on his face and the hair on his head was clotted.

He looked almost the way he'd looked when Dikar first found him, a starved Beast-man in the woods below the Mountain. "You were right, Dikar. The Asafrics laid a trap for us and we marched the army right into it."

"The army, Walt! All killed?"

"Many. Too many. But according to the reports I've been gathering, not nearly as many as we thought at first. Our men dispersed as soon as it began, found gullies like this one, caves, other shelter. Even those who could not find better cover than the woods were so scattered that each bomb or shell caught only two or three.

"We've lost only about six or seven hundred men. That still leaves us nearly five thousand effectives, but we can no longer count on surprising the Asafrics, so a frontal assault on those natural ramparts cannot possibly succeed."

Dikar didn't understand all Walt's words, but he knew what he meant. "Then we've given up. We're licked."

"Not quite." The back of Walt's hand scraped at the stiff hair on his chin. "There's still one slim chance. That's why Fenton sent me through that hell-fire to look for you."

"Why for me?"

"Because if anyone can make good that chance, it's you and your Bunch. Look!" Walt pointed up and up to where Dikar had seen the guns flash this morning. "You see that fold in the mountains, right there?"

"Yes." The flashes were still there, bright against the dark green of the high woods, and the thunder of the guns still rolled down from there. "Sure I do."

"That's Newfound Gap, the highest point on the highway that goes over these mountains. When the Smokies were made a National Park, the engineers built a wide, level place there where hundreds of cars could park while their passengers looked over the view.

"The Asafrics have emplaced their biggest guns there, monsters with a fifty-mile range, commanding not only all this valley, but the whole length of the highway up which we'd planned to steal tonight, to make our surprise attack."

"I know," Dikar broke in. "But now the Asafrics will be watchin' for us an' kill us all if we try it."

"EXACTLY. THEY have the range of every inch of it. On the other hand, if we can capture those guns we can still snatch victory from defeat. You see, Dikar, we could swing them around and shell the enemy out of the reaches between the Smokies and the Cumberland Plateau. That would make it possible for our Army of the Tennessee to break through, join up with us and clean up the rest of the enemy forces in the mountains."

"How're we goin' to capture those guns if we can't get up to 'em?"

"Look there to the left." Dikar's eyes went along the line of soaring, dark green peaks up from which drifted a blue-gray haze like smoke from hidden fires. "There. That's Clingman's Dome."

So high was the mountain Walt pointed to that, far above, a cloud blanked out its middle half and its top seemed a monstrous, impossible island floating in the sky.

"It rises a thousand feet above Newfound Gap," Walt was saying, "and there is another battery emplaced there, of automatic air-craft guns, like the archy you fired from the roof when we captured West Point. They're toys compared to the ones at the Gap, but they're placed just right to annihilate the crews of the big ones."

A chill prickle ran up and down Dikar's backbone, but he only said, very quiet, "All right, Walt. We'll go up there an'—"

"Wait!" Walt's voice was sharp. "Wait till I finish." Dikar had a queer feeling that his friend didn't want him to go up there with the Bunch. "General Fenton wants you to understand exactly what the job means."

"I don't care—"

"Listen, Dikar," Marilee's clear, sweet voice interrupted. "Listen to what Walt has to say." She was standing close to them, and the others of the Bunch were gathered around. The Boys' eyes were shining and eager but the Girls' eyes, watching Walt, were shadowed.

"A ridge, along which runs an automobile road, connects Newfound Gap, to the north-east of it, with Clingman's Dome. Its eastern slope, the one toward us, and the southern are comparatively gentle and easy to climb, and so are certainly carefully watched. The Dome's western side, however, is a steep cliff almost as unscalable as that around the base of your Mountain—"

"And you think they won't be watchin' that side. But they'd be crazy not to, if they know we're around."

"If they know our army is in the vicinity they'll certainly be on the alert. But suppose we pretend to withdraw? Suppose, now that the planes have left, we send numbers of men to expose themselves on roads visible from the mountain-tops, apparently fleeing from the valley—"

"The Asafrics will think there's lots more runnin' away, in the woods where they can't see 'em. An' they'll get a little careless—"

"Exactly. If the ruse should succeed it might barely be possible for a little band of men to reach the summit of Clingman's Dome unobserved under cover of the night.

"*Might* be, Dikar," Walt repeated. "But if you try it, you will be climbing in darkness along ledges so narrow that they will barely give you foothold, ledges clinging to the side of precipices that slant outward to push you off.

"Above you will be Blacks and their hearin' is as keen as an animal's. An exclamation, the clink of metal against rock, even a stone dislodged would warn them of your approach. If you're shot at and only wounded, if you make a single misstep, you will fall three thousand feet or more into what they call hereabouts a Rhododendron Hell, a tangled and trackless thicket."

Walt pulled in breath, put a hand on Dikar's arm. "The chances are a thousand to one against your ever reaching the top, my boy, and even if you do, the odds are almost as great that you'll die up there."

Again he stopped talking for a moment, lines cutting deep into his gaunt cheeks. "That's why General Fenton will not order you to make the try, but has sent me only to ask if you will?"

DIKAR LOOKED up again at the misty island in the sky, looked down at Walt. The sun was warm on his skin. The smells of the woods were warm in his nostrils and he knew in that moment how good life was.

He said slowly, "You know what my answer would be if I had to answer only for myself. But this is somethin' you ask of the Bunch, the Boys to climb up there an' the Girls to wait here below, wonderin' what is happenin' to us up there in the dark. And so I cannot answer, but only the Bunch can answer, in Council."

Dikar saw in Marilee's eyes that what he was saying was the right thing to say. He wet his lips and said, a little louder: "I call a Council. Right here an' now, I call a Council of the Bunch."

Walt pushed back out of the crowd, and the Bunch crowded in close. Dikar looked around him at the Boys and Girls whom the Old Ones had made him Boss of a long time ago. He thought of all their years on the Mountain, and how happy their life on the Mountain had been, and how he'd led them down off the Mountain because of his dream that in them was the hope of a new tomorrow for America.

In that moment between breath and breath, Dikar thought of all the Councils he had called on the Mountain, and all the Councils he'd called in the Far Land after he'd led the Bunch down off the Mountain. This was the strangest Council he'd ever called, here on this torn, red earth with the thunder of the Asafric guns rolling overhead, the Asafric shells bursting all around.

And then Dikar had taken his breath, and was talking again. "You have all heard Walt. You know what it is we are asked to do. You know what it means to America if we can do it, an' you know what it means to us if we fail. What answer do we give Walt to take back to the President of America?"

"What answer could we give?" Johnstone, black-haired, black-bearded, came back at once. "We do it, of course. What say, Boys? Am I right?"

"Right!" yelled Carlberger and Patmara and hook-nosed Abestein. "Right," yelled the Boys, every one of them, and then Franksmith, thin and tall and red-bearded, was saying: "Settled, Dikar. We do it. And you knew all the time that's what we'd say."

Dikar saw Bessalton's hand start out to catch hold of Franksmith and then pull back inside her cloak of black hair, and he saw the look that had come into Bessalton's eyes. "Yes, Franksmith," Dikar said. "I knew what you Boys would say. But the Girls have full voice in the Council of the Bunch, an' I have not heard from 'em. What do the Girls say, Bessalton?"

Bessalton's hair was black as night in the deep woods, but her face was white as new snow with the sun on it. Her lips were gray as they moved and no sound came from them, and then words came from them.

"The Girls say there is only one answer to what is asked, Dikar. The Girls say that it must be done."

And the faces of all the Girls were white and drawn, their

eyes dark with agony, but not one Girl spoke up to say that Bessalton did not talk for her.

CHAPTER 3
CLIMB TO JEOPARDY

D IKAR HELD tight to a knob of rock, just over his head. His weight was all on the ball of his right foot, clinging to a two-inch shelf of rock. His left leg swung free over emptiness.

If Dikar looked down, he would see the night-filled emptiness fall away from him, down and down to a black sough of wind in trees and brush. If Dikar looked down, he would let go. He would follow his look, down into the black depths.

The muscles of his neck tightened to keep his head from turning to look down. All his strength was in his neck, and there was no strength in him to move his left leg, which swung back and out over the awful depths.

For an endless time Dikar hung like that, between the depths and the overhang of the terrible cliff above him.

There was no moon, but when Dikar had climbed up out of the brush tangle that was so terribly far below now, when he'd climbed up above the black whisper of wind in the treetops, starlight had glimmered on the face of the high sheer cliff. Just enough light there had been for Dikar, climbing first, to find a ledge, a slope of earth, ledge again and slope of broken, rotted bits of stone.

Slowly, painfully, Dikar had led the Boys up the western face of Clingman's Dome. Ledge, and slope, ledge and slope again, they had climbed, starlight laying their shadows black on the glimmering rock. Slowly they'd climbed, hardly daring to breathe, almost not daring to move lest the next reach of hand or foot send some little stone rattling down the mountainside and give them away to the Asafrics above.

Death waiting above, death waiting below, Dikar had led the

Boys up until this last ledge suddenly had narrowed to give hold only to the balls of his feet, and then had melted into an out-thrust of rock, like a rounded wall corner.

Dikar could see nothing beyond the outthrust of rock. Above him the cliff slanted outward, as if to push him off, and there was no foothold on it, only the one little knob which his right hand clutched. There was no way to go but back.

Before Dikar could get the Boys back to where there was a choice of path, the dawn would be here to show them to the Asafrics. To go back was to give up.

Holding on to the knob of rock, Dikar groped with his left hand along the rocky outthrust, around its bulge and he found a tiny crack into which his fingernails could catch. Pulling in breath, Dikar swung his left leg back, off the two-inch ledge, to get it around the bulge.

In that moment the pull of the black depths took hold of Dikar and his strength ran out of him. He hung against the side of the cliff, and along the ledge beyond him, the Boys waited, unable to help him.

THE COLD of the high places lay icy against Dikar's skin. To make the climb, the Boys had taken off their fawn-skins; they wore only the little aprons of plaited twigs they'd worn on their Mountain, and thrust into the belts of the aprons were long, sharp knives sheathed by leather.

Rifles would have been too clumsy to carry on that climb. The little guns called revolvers would have been too heavy. Knives were better, anyway, for what they had to do at the end of the climb.

But this was the end of the climb, Dikar thought with a quick surge of fear. For slowly, surely, against his strength, against the tight cords in his neck, his head was turning!

For a moment Dikar kept his head from slanting down to look into the black depths. For a last, fleeting instant he looked, instead, into a velvet-black sky.

They were so close, the stars, that Dikar had only to reach

out to touch them. They were the same stars that had been close and friendly when he'd gone up to the tall oak on the very top of his Mountain, to dream how some day he would lead the Bunch down off the Mountain to free America.

This was the end of his dream, this fall into the black depths.

No! Suddenly Dikar had strength to break the pull. His head snapped back to the cliff. His left leg swung against the out-thrust of rock, groped around it. His toes found something, an edge of stone, slid over and found a hold, a place for his foot as far in as it would go with his thigh hard against the rocky bulge.

Dikar's weight went from right foot to left. The nails of his left hand pried into the crack. His right hand let go. Somehow Dikar was around the corner. He was safe on a wide, almost level shelf of rock. Held breath went out of him and he dropped to his knees, clammy with sweat in spite of the cold.

Dikar looked up. Above him, not twenty feet, was a waver-ing red glow of firelight and against the glow a sharp-edged black mass.

That was the top of Clingman's Dome. Up to it sloped clean rock on which bare feet would make no sound, an ascent that would be like a level road after what Dikar had climbed tonight.

Like a level road, but it was clean of brush or grass or even boulder to hide behind, and it was pale in the starlight. The smallest creature moving on it would stand out plain, and nothing could live in the sweep of gunfire from up there.

A FAINT rub of flesh on stone turned Dikar to the fold of rock around which he'd come. A hand groped into sight. Dikar's fingers grabbed its wrist, held tight. A bare foot crept around the stone. Dikar had hold of that, was guiding it to firm hold. Franksmith came around the rock corner into Dikar's arms. Franksmith's pale face twitched and his gray lips started to open, but Dikar's palm was on his mouth, stopping the words. Dikar pointed to the glow of the Asafrics' fire above to show Franksmith why it was not safe to speak.

And then another hand came around the rock-corner; Dikar helped Alfoster to safety. One by one they came around the bulge, Abestein, Louvance, Patmara, one by one, till Dikar was gesturing the sixteenth, Johnstone, to lie flat and silent on the rock beside the others.

Dikar was down on the rock, his fingers were on the hilt of the knife to make sure it was loose in its sheath. He was stealing up the starlit slope, the Boys following behind.

They made no more sound than the bat makes, flitting through the gray dusk, but in Dikar's ears the drum of his blood was so loud that he was sure the Asafrics must hear it, and where he crawled the stone was ruddy with firelight.

All of a sudden it was black with a shadow. Dikar froze. The shadow was thrown by a sort of low wall of rocks to which he'd come.

He waved for the Boys to come up into the shielding blackness, knew that they obeyed because he could see the blackness take them. He moved to the wall, was motionless again except for his head and shoulders, which lifted, very slowly. Dikar's eyes came above the top of the wall and his head stopped lifting.

The fire was a big pile of red-glowing logs in the middle of a broad space of level ground. The wall ran all around the edge of the space, but on Dikar's left it was broken by a gap through which he could see the beginning of the road to Newfound Gap. Near this a low stone house slept, door closed, windows glinting with reflection of the fire.

Beyond the fire, long and slim and black, the barrels of the eight anti-aircraft guns slanted up against a vast and empty sky. Then there was the long, low line of the wall.

Now something blotched the sharp line of the wall. It was the head and shoulders of a man. The firelight did not reach him, so he was just a black shape to Dikar, but the little hairs at the back of Dikar's neck bristled as his nose caught the smell of him.

The smell of Hashamoto's Black soldiers.

Dikar made out another, and another, and their backs were to him. Each leaned on the wall, peering down over it. Dikar saw that each held a rifle on the wall in front of him, his hands on it. There were twelve and they stood all along three sides of the wall, but there were none on this fourth side. As Walt had thought, they were sure that the terrible west side of the Dome would keep anyone from coming up here

DIKAR'S LIPS twisted in a humorless smile. He beckoned the Boys up to him. He let them get a glimpse of the Asafrics, waved them down below the wall again, pointed to each of the Boys, pointed for each in the direction of an Asafric. Nods told him that they understood.

Dikar pulled his knife from its sheath, and drew a long breath. He came up straight, leaped the wall. He was running silent-footed across the space within. From the corner of his eye he saw the silent, shadowy shapes of the Boys running across the space, fanning out, the firelight glinting on the blades of their knives.

Dikar went past an archie, was close on top of the Asafric he'd picked for himself. His right arm swung up, down. The blade of his knife slid into flesh, scraped bone. Without a sound, the Black pitched over the wall.

Dikar's knife was crimson, but the firelight didn't make it so. A scream, like a trapped rabbit's shrilled in his ears. Dikar twisted to it, saw an Asafric wheeling around to Carlberger, saw the Asafric's rifle swinging like a club.

As Dikar leaped, there was a cracking sound. Carlberger, dropping, had a misshaped something where his head had been. The Asafric screamed again, eyes white in the shiny black round of his face, teeth white between thick, purplish lips. Dikar's knife sliced across the black throat. A new, bright light was all around Dikar as the Black fell.

The new light came from the door of the stone house, open now. It framed a squat yellow man in uniform of Asafric green, with undressed Blacks crowding behind him. The slant eyes saw Dikar in that same moment and the officer's revolver spoke. Dikar dropped, hit the ground with a thud.

CHAPTER 4
OUT OF THE NIGHT...

THE YELLOW officer yelled something and came out of the door, his revolver barking. A Black came out behind him, rifle to shoulder. Another, and another.

Dikar had dropped behind the iron bottom part of an archie in the eye-wink before the officer had shot. He saw a bronzed shape lunge for the Yellow, saw the Boy knocked down by a red streak from the rifle of one of the Blacks. There was something hard under Dikar—the rifle of the Asafric whose throat he'd cut. Dikar grabbed it up, saw the Blacks spreading out from the door of the little house, got the butt of the gun to his shoulder, sighting the Yellow officer, and pulled the trigger.

The officer dropped. "Rifles!" Dikar yelled. "Grab the rifles of the Asafrics you've killed." He brought down a Black, plain against the bright light from the house-door. A bullet spanged on the iron of the archy—another.

Then suddenly the bright light was gone. The door had slammed closed on the Blacks who'd dived back into the house.

"Hurray!" A clear, high voice cried. "Hurray, fellers. We've won," Louvance came out from behind an archy, and an instant later he was knocked down by a red streak from the dark wall of the stone house.

"Cover!" Dikar yelled. "Keep your cover! They're shootin' through holes in the wall of the house! They can see us an' shoot us, but we can't get at 'em. Hold your shooting till you have a mark."

All of a sudden it was quiet there on top of Clingman's Dome, so quiet that Dikar could hear the hard breathing of someone who'd been hurt. He saw that the breathing came from the first Boy who'd been shot.

But the Boy wasn't where he'd fallen when the Yellow officer had shot him. He'd dragged himself much nearer the house, and there was a dark, glistening path on the ground from where he had fallen.

Shots sounded dully inside the house, but the Boy hung against the wall, and he was doing something with his knife. He was cutting wires, Dikar saw, that ran up along the wall to the roof and then straight out from the roof, overhead, to a pole on the road to Newfound Gap.

More dull shot-sounds, but no red flashes. That meant they were coming from a hole in the wall right up against the Boy's body. The Boy slid down along the wall and lay still at its foot. But the wires hung loose now, cut through.

"WHAT—WHAT DID he do that for?" a sick-sounding voice asked, right behind Dikar. "What did he do that crazy thing for?"

Dikar looked back, saw that Johnstone had crawled to him in the black shadow of the wall that ran around this space. "Not crazy," Dikar said. "Not crazy at all. Don't you see what kind of wires those are?"

There was a queer sound in Johnstone's throat, and then, "Yeah. They're tel'phone wires—"

"To the Gap. He cut 'em to keep the Asafrics here from callin' for help from there. We can't get at 'em in that house, an' they can't get at us as long as we hide behind these big guns, but they could have held us here till soldiers from Newfound Gap came. Whoever that was, he could have laid still an' maybe been safe, but he gave his life to save the rest of us. It was a brave thing. Who was he?"

"Franksmith." Johnstone said, low-voiced.

Dikar thought of the way Bessalton's hand had come out to take hold of Franksmith. He thought of the look in Bessalton's eyes as her gray lips had made the words, "The Girls say it must be done."

"What do we do now, Dikar?" Johnstone was asking. "We're pretty safe as long as we stay behind these archies, but we can't shoot 'em at Newfound Gap unless we go out in front of 'em, an' we don't dare do that so long as there are any Asafrics left in that house."

"Right. So we've got to get 'em out of there." Dikar made up his mind. "Listen, Johnstone. You crawl back along the wall an' tell all the Boys to start shootin' at the house the minute I whistle."

Johnstone was gone and Dikar, crouched behind the archy, started counting. While he counted to twenty he carefully thought over all that Walt had told him about shooting off the archies. Then he made himself not think at all while he counted to thirty, to forty, only watch how a faint grayness was coming into the sky, how the stars were paling. But as he counted forty-five, Dikar thought about Marilee....

"Fifty," he counted and whistled, loud and shrill. The Boys' rifles crashed, their red fire streaking the night. Dikar darted out from behind the cover of the gun and jumped up into the little iron seat fastened to it, right in full view of the Asafrics in the house. He grabbed a wheel and turned it, and the gun started to move, but a bullet spanged on the gun's iron, another sang over his head, and a third fanned his cheek.

The gun was turning on its mount, but it was turning slowly, and Dikar was a fair mark from the stone house. He pulled at an iron stick which made the gun's barrel start coming down as it turned. Something plucked at his left arm, and something burned across his thigh. The gun had turned so that it was between Dikar and the little stone house, and its barrel was all the way down now, so that it pointed right at the little house.

Dikar pulled another little iron stick.

The archy jumped under Dikar. Thunder deafened Dikar, blinded him. The archy jumped again, and again. Dikar pulled the stick again. The little house wasn't there any more. All that was there was a few tumbled stones, and a big hole in the wall.

"All right, Boys!" Dikar yelled, and he was still so deaf that he couldn't hear himself yell. "All right. Gun crews to your places, quick! Aim down that road to Newfound Gap." Then quietly, as if he were falling asleep, he leaned sidewise and fell out of the little iron seat, fell smiling into the dark.

CHAPTER 5
MONUMENT BETWEEN BATTLES

THE EARTH was springy under Dikar's running feet and its coolness was good to feel. The woods smells—the brown smell of the earth, the green smell of brush and leaves—were good in Dikar's nostrils. Best of all was the silver, happy sound of Marilee's laughter as she ran from him, hid just ahead by a green tangle of brush.

All of a sudden Marilee's laughter ended.

Dikar broke through the green curtain that hid Marilee. He stopped short. The brush had been cleared away here, so that he could see farther through the gray-brown tree-trunks than Marilee could have run, but there was no Marilee to be seen, not even the press of her feet on the moss.

Dikar stood very still, a muscle twitching in his cheek. A line of excited ants hurried through the moss near his feet, each carrying a white egg in its strong jaws. A green snake slid lithely out from behind a gnarled elbow of root, its tiny black eyes bright in its three-cornered, flat head. A bump on a stone was a warty toad, so still that it might be dead. A fly flitted too near it and the toad's tongue flicked out of, in again to its wide, ugly mouth. The fly was gone.

Over Dikar's head a squirrel chrrred, scolding. Dikar grinned

*Then, before Dikar
could fire, he was
seized from behind.*

and his knees bent, straightened to send him
flying upward. His hands, upflung, caught an
oak's sturdy bough. His feet found hold on the bough. Dikar
stood erect, was climbing the swaying ladder of leafy branches
quick and sure as any squirrel. In the green heart of the tree,
Marilee was curled on a branching fork, her gray eyes dancing.

Her hair was a silken glory about her, but only her skirt of
plaited grasses, her breast-circlets of woven flowers, covered her
brown loveliness. Legs astraddle on a bough beneath, Dikar
plucked his mate from her perch and held her, arm-cradled,
over empty space.

"I'm going to drop you," he growled, deep in his chest, "for
thinkin' you could get away from me. Hey! Let go my beard."

She only pulled its golden hairs harder as she laughed. "Fins!"
Dikar cried. "Fins! I won't drop you." He settled down in the
fork where she had been, held Marilee nestling against him.

"Oh, Dikar." Marilee's voice lifted with happiness. "You
jumped up here like you'd never been hurt. You're all well again,
Dikar!"

"Didn't I tell you I was?"

"Yes, you did. But I couldn't believe it. I kept thinkin' how the doctor said, when you were carried down here to Norrisdam a month ago, that you wouldn't even be able to walk till the end of the summer."

"Aw! What do those fool doctors know? We got along pretty good without 'em, all the time we lived on our Mountain, didn't we? They don't know anythin'."

"Silly!" Marilee frowned. "Doctors are awful smart. They know a lot—"

"But they don't know as much as you do about the roots and grasses that heal hurts. If it hadn't been for you I'd be still layin' on that bed."

"I'll never forget how you looked, all bloody and torn with the Asafric bullets—"

"That first week must have been a bad time for you. I'm sorry you had such a bad time on account of me." He gathered her closer to him. "Let me show you how sorry I am, Marilee. Marilee." He bent his face to hers.

FOR A long time she would not untwine her arms from around him, but at last she let him put her on the bough beside him. He leaned back against the bark of the tree and she nestled close against him.

"Ah," Marilee sighed, eyelids drooped, moist-red lips wistful. "This is grand, just you an' me alone together. It's like we were back in our tree on the tiptop of the Mountain, lookin' out at the Far Land an' wonderin' what was there."

A shadow stole over Dikar's face. "Maybe I shouldn't ever have led the Bunch down off the Mountain." This was the thought that had been bothering him. "Maybe I was wrong to do that. Look, Marilee. If I hadn't little Carlberger would be alive today, an' Louvance an'—"

"An' Normanfenton would be skin an' bones dried by the wind, Dikar, hangin' in chains from the top of the Empire State Buildin' in New York." Marilee pulled a leaf from a twig. "Walt would still be a Beast Man, dirty an' starvin' in the woods below our Mountain, or maybe the Asafrics would have caught him an' put him in one of their cages in which a man can neither stand up nor sit nor lie down.

"Johndawson— Oh! You know as well as I do that if you had not led the Bunch off the Mountain, there would not be anyone fightin' to make America free."

"We were free on our Mountain, Marilee. We lived our own happy life there, an' nobody bothered us."

"Yes." Marilee pulled little bits from the leaf, let them flutter from long, slim fingers. "Yes, Dikar. We were free. We were happy. We could not hear the whips of the Asafrics on the backs of white men an' women. We could not see the people herded in filth an' sufferin' inside the barbed wire of the concentration camps.

"We were not bein' driven by the guns an' the kicks of the Blacks to slave in factories an' mines, makin' things not for ourselves but our masters. All of those things and lots more, lots worse, were happenin' in the Far Land, but on our Mountain we lived the good life."

"We earned it, Marilee. We worked hard for it, all the years since the Old Ones brought us to the Mountain."

"An' gave us the Musts an' Must-Nots, the Law, by which we should live happy—then died so that we could live free. When the Asafric soldiers came to the Mountain, the Old Ones did not run away an' hide in the woods, did they? They went down off the Mountain to meet the Asafrics. They gave their lives gladly.

"The Old Ones had heard the voice," she went on, "that you yourself told me about in our tree on the tiptop of the Mountain. They had heard the Voice that came into a dark place under the ground where mothers huddled their little children to them while the thunder of bombs rumbled overhead. They'd heard it sayin': 'In these little children lies America's last, faint hope of—of a—'" Marilee hesitated, looked at Dikar, her brows knitting.

" 'Of a tomorrow,' " Dikar helped her, " 'when democracy, liberty, freedom,' " all of a sudden his voice was clear and certain, " 'shall reconquer the green an' pleasant fields that tonight lie devastated.' "

"YOU DO remember!" Marilee's face was alight again. "You do remember the Voice you heard a long time ago in a dream. You have not forgotten it."

"You have made me remember it, my sweet." Dikar knew now why Marilee had brought him up here into this tree that was so like the tree where he'd told her, first of all the Bunch, about his dream and the Voice in it. "I had forgotten. This morning, when for the first time since Clingman's Dome I came to Brekfes with the Bunch an' looked around the table, what I saw made me forget my dream."

"What you saw?"

Dikar's hands closed into fists, so tight their knuckles whitened. "Eight Boys only, Marilee, are left of the twenty-six I led down off the Mountain. Nine, countin' myself. The rest are dead an' buried."

"There was a smile on Franksmith's face when we buried him, Dikar. His body was all torn with the Asafric's bullets, but there was a happy, peaceful smile on his face. You know there was."

"There was no smile on Bessalton's face, this mornin'. There was no light in her eyes. She sat there, white an' silent, an' if Alicekane had not kept after her, she would not have eaten a bite."

"There are smiles, Dikar, on the faces of hundreds and hundreds of women, all across this land. They have hope now, but they would not have it if you had not led Franksmith an' Bessalton an' all the rest of the Bunch down from the Mountain. Did you do wrong, Dikar, when you did that?"

"No, Marilee; I did right. I did—"

Dikar broke off and his head canted, listening to a call from somewhere below. "Helloooo. Helloooo, Dikar." It was coming nearer. "Dikar. Where are you? Helloooo."

Dikar dropped down to the tree's lowest bough, pushed aside leaves from his face. "Here, Nedsmall." Bushes were threshing, down there. "Here I am." The toad hopped from his stone and the green snake flicked back behind its elbow of root. "What is it? What do you want?"

The bushes parted and Nedsmall came into sight. "Oh Dikar." He looked up and sunbeams danced on his freckle-dusted, impish face. "I been lookin' all over for you." He was the small-est of the Boys. "Walt sent word you're wanted at Headquarters. You're to meet him on top of the dam in half an hour."

"Dikar's wanted at Headquarters?" Marilee was alongside Dikar on the bough, the two standing there without using their hands to hold on, comfortable as if on the ground. "What for?"

"I wasn't told," Nedsmall shrugged. "But I know what I hope," He looked excited. "I'm tired hangin' around here doin' nothin'. I hope they got another job for us to do."

Dikar heard Marilee's breath pull in. "All right, Nedsmall," he said. "Thanks for tellin' me." He watched the youngster run off.

"So soon," Marilee whispered. "Oh Dikar. Why couldn't they let me have you for myself a little while longer."

Dikar smiled at her, but there was no smile in his blue eyes. "You could have had me all for yourself, all the time, if we'd stayed on the Mountain. But I seem to remember your sayin' that it would have been wrong for us to have stayed there."

"I said that." Marilee laid her little hand on Dikar's arm and her fingers were icy cold, trembling. "An' I meant it. I was talkin' to the Boss of the Bunch then. Just now I'm thinkin' about my mate."

CHAPTER 6
LOOK ON MY WORK...

NORRISDAM WAS a white stone wall that men had built, joining one great hill to another. Its top was wide enough for ten men to walk abreast, and its bottom was so far below the top that men down there looked no bigger to Dikar than his thumb.

That was on one side. On the other side was water, a great lake of water stretching back between green, forested hills as far as Dikar could see. "The lake is as deep as the dam is high," Walt told Dikar as they walked along the top of the dam. "But before the dam was built there was only a little muddy river way down there on what is now the lake's bottom."

"Why was this dam built?" Dikar asked. "Why did they make the lake here?"

"Because the farm lands of eight states, from the mountains of Virginia to the Ohio River, were being washed away by the spring floods, and in the summer what soils the floods had not washed away was cracked and thirsty with drought, the crops yellow and dying.

"So engineers built this dam, and others like it. It was a great thing they did, Dikar. They harnessed the floods and the storms and gave the people of these states fertile fields and cheap power. They gave the people a better life."

"Men built mountains like this," Dikar's forehead was wrinkled, his eyes puzzled, "so that they could have a better life?"

"Exactly."

"They were smart enough an' strong enough to do that," Dikar said, as if to himself. He stared at Walt. "Then why couldn't they keep hold of the mountains they built? Why couldn't they go on making their life better and better? What happened to them?"

Walt shrugged with a bitter smile. "I don't know," he said. "The men who built the mountains were engineers. But the men who had the job of making the better life work and keep on working—they were statesmen." He started walking faster. "We haven't got time to talk about that now, Dikar. General Fenton's waiting for us."

They came to the end of the road along the dam's top and hurried across a wide, stone-paved field where hundreds of men in gray-blue uniforms were lounged. Dikar was thinking that maybe if people had taken time to talk about things like this before it was too late, things would be different now. But he didn't say the thought aloud, because they were going into the stone building that was called Headquarters here at Norrisdam.

NORMANFENTON STOOD looking out of a high, round-topped window when Walt and Dikar came into his room. He seemed thinner than the last time Dikar had seen him, at Wespoint, but he was still very tall, and his long legs and long arms still looked as if they'd been hitched on to his body in a hurry and not very carefully.

But when Normanfenton turned and Dikar saw his face once more, Dikar forgot how clumsy his body was.

His great head, with its gray-threaded, straggly black beard, seemed somehow too big for that ungainly body. Gaunt cheeks were molded by bones very near the surface of the skin, and the skin was scribbled over with a tracery of wrinkles, fine as the threads of a spider-web. Under a broad and thoughtful forehead, eyes were deep-sunken and somber.

In Normanfenton's eyes was pain, and a dreadful tiredness, but in them there was also the soft light of a vision seen far off. Seeing Dikar, he smiled and his whole face seemed to brighten with a warm and tender welcome.

"Ah, my boy." His voice was not very loud, but it seemed to fill the big room as he held out a gnarled hand to take Dikar's strong, brown one. "I have not had the opportunity yet to thank you for what you and your—Bunch did up there on the roof of the Smokies."

"I—uh—" Dikar swallowed, shifted from one foot to the other. "It was nothing, Norman—Mr. President." He remembered just in time how he was supposed to talk to Normanfenton. "Anybody could have done the same thing."

"I don't agree. Perhaps others might have had the same will and courage, but you possess certain unique skills that none without your peculiar background can match. And it is of those particular skills that we have need again, or I should not have sent for you as soon as I heard that you had recovered from your wounds."

"What job do you want me to do?" Dikar asked. "Tell me."

The warm smile flickered in Normanfenton's eyes and then faded. "Captain Bennet." He looked at Walt. "Will you be good enough to send the guard outside beyond earshot and remain at the door yourself so that we can be absolutely certain there are no eavesdroppers?" Walt saluted and obeyed. "When we were on the Mountain together, Dikar," said the President, turning to him again, "I think I taught you something about maps. Am I right?"

"Yes. You taught me a little then an' Walt—Cap'n Bennet— has taught me a lot more since."

"Good. That will make my explanation easier. Look here." Normanfenton took Dikar's arm, led him to the wall to the left of the window. "This is a map of the southern quarter of the United States, Mexico and Central America."

It was a bigger map than any Dikar had ever seen, and he thought it a shame someone had stuck a lot of different colored pins into it. "I didn't think we would be concerned with that region for a long time yet," Normanfenton went on. "But I've had some news this morning—" He stopped, sighed. His fingers tightened on Dikar's arm. "Bad news, Dikar. Danger threatens our cause. A graver danger than ever before."

Normanfenton put his forefinger on the map. "I'm going to

send you down there, my boy. It will be a miracle if you can get there. It will be a miracle if you can accomplish what I'm sending you to do. But the cause of freedom can be saved only by a miracle now."

IT WAS very quiet in the room, so quiet that as Normanfenton stopped talking for a minute, Dikar could hear the rustling of the ivy that grew thick on the wall outside, the lap, lap of the lake's waters close to the bottom of that wall.

And the slow throb of the blood in his ears.

"Only by a miracle," Normanfenton sighed, "and so very many things can happen to prevent you from working that miracle. If what I'm going to tell you should leak out to the enemy—"The look of pain deepened in his face. "We must take every precaution that it shall not. You must repeat what you are about to hear to no one, Dikar. Not even to that lovely wife of yours. Do you understand?"

"I understand," Dikar said through cold lips, but he didn't. He was wondering why Normanfenton didn't want him to tell Marilee.

"Not that I don't trust her as much as I do you, but a single inadvertent remark— There are spies in camp here, my boy." The look of pain deepened on the Leader's face. "Matters have reached the enemy that only someone on my personal staff could have known. This matter *must not.*"

He turned abruptly to the map. "Now that's understood, I'll explain what it's all about. First, perhaps, I had better tell you how things stand now."

Dikar moved to the other side of the President so that he could see better.

"After we took Newfound Gap," Normanfenton began, "we—" Dikar whirled away from him. Face suddenly white, he bounded to the window, leaned out.

He'd heard, from outside here, a sudden gasp, quickly cut off, and a threshing of leaves. Someone clinging to the vine to listen had missed his hold and grabbed for a better one to save himself from falling.

He hadn't saved himself! There was a splash from the water below. Dikar saw a blurred form deep under the lake's surface. Then he had vaulted the sill and he was plunging down into the icy waters of Norris Lake.

CHAPTER 7

HOPE LIES IN THE JUNGLE

A History of the Asiatic-African World Hegemony, Zafir Uscudan, LL.D (Singapore) F.I.H.S., etc. Third Edition, vol. 3. Chap. XXVII p 988.

...Inspired by the manner in which Dikar and his Bunch had, at fearful cost, used their woodland skills to breach the Asafrics' mountain breastworks and made possible the union of the two branches of his Eastern Army across the Tennessee Valley, General Norman Fenton resolved to attempt a similar junction between these forces and the rebel Americans who had gained virtual control of the central Mid-west.

To this ambitious project, Viceroy Yee Hashamoto's gunboat patrol of the Mississippi interposed a formidable obstacle. Following the pattern of the tactics by which the Great Uprising had grown from a mere rioting of a few disaffected slaves to the dignity of a major insurrection, President Fenton initiated simultaneous feints-in-force toward Chicago and New Orleans, contriving, through patriots posing as renegade Mudskins, to get word of these to Hashamoto.

The latter at once concentrated his strength on the threatened cities, setting up traps like the one at the Great Smoky Mountains that the Americans had escaped only through Dikar's brilliant exploit.

On May 23rd–24th, Fenton delivered his genuine assault against the weakened forces that had been left to hold Cairo,

Illinois, and its vicinity. His stratagem was completely success-
ful. The Mississippi was crossed, and penetration of the Ozark
Plateau from the bridgehead thus established.

In the face of these repeated defeats, Yee Hashamoto still
sedulously concealed from the Asiatic-African Confederation's
Supreme Command at home any knowledge that he was in
difficulty. To explain why, we must refer back to Chapter II of
this History.

The reader will recall that here we discussed the character-
istics that so well fitted the leaders of the Asafric Cabal for the
program of world conquest on which they embarked when
"Axis diplomacy", having invited them as allies into the arena
of *Welt Politik,* revealed to them the rotten beams behind the
facade of vaunted white supremacy. We also pointed out a
psychological weakness, the Oriental preoccupation with "Face."

HASHAMOTO HAD only to draw upon the Confederation's
tremendous military resources to crush the American Uprising,
even now. But by so doing, he must admit his own failure. He
must admit that a slave whom he had paraded through the
countryside, naked and in chains, had out-maneuvered, out-
generaled him. He would "lose face." This was unthinkable.

It was also inevitable, unless he took strong measures at once.
There were increasingly urgent demands from across the Pacific
for explanation of why the flow of cargoes from his bailiwick
was so materially dwindling, and the Viceroy was running out
of excuses. With each victory, the numbers of the insurrectionists were growing as liberated slaves flocked to their standards.
He could not very much longer keep his secret.

From this dilemma, Hashamoto saw one means of escape.
The Asafrics' first incursion into the Western Hemisphere had
been by way of South America. That continent was still docile.
Hashamoto had two tank divisions guarding the Panama Canal,
but no threat there was possible.

They were the reinforcements he needed. All he had to do
was bring one of those divisions up through Central America

and Mexico. Using Texas as a springboard, they could strike the Americans on their exposed southern flank, drive north through the Central Plain and then, facing westward, herd the insurrectionists toward the Rockies.

In the latter range would be waiting the West Coast troops that had so far maintained undisputed control over California and the Columbia River Valley. Caught between two fires, a full half of Fenton's forces would be destroyed.

Meanwhile, relieved of concern with the prairies, Hashamoto's present contingents would be equal to the task of annihilating the remaining rebels.

Viceroy Yee Hashamoto's wireless flashed the orders. Perhaps he was not aware that the Americans could intercept and decode the message. Perhaps he did not care. It was a good plan, and even if General Norman Fenton, in his headquarters at Norris Dam, knew about it, he was helpless to defeat it. . . .

"IT'S A good plan"—there was deep worry in Normanfenton's voice—"that of Hashamoto's." Dikar shivered a little. The fawn-skin draped over his left shoulder and around his brown, strong body was still chilly-wet from the lake, though he'd been listening so long that the water had dried from his thighs and his legs.

"We will be helpless against his tanks, once they reach Texas. Here." The General's bony finger rested on the map, just above where the blue that meant water took a big bite out of the bottom of the United States. "They've got to be stopped before they get this far, and that's what I'm putting up to you."

"To *me!*" Dikar gasped. "How can I stop 'em?"

Dikar could swim like a fish, but he'd been blinded by the splash of his own wild dive out of the window and before he could see again, the spy who had been listening under it had swum too far under water to be seen.

"My only hope, son," Normanfenton answered him, "that they can be stopped rests on you."

The funny thing was that though some of the Boys and Girls

of the Bunch had been in swimming where the woods came down to the shore on the other side of Norris Lake, none of them had seen any stranger come up out of it. Dikar had sent the Bunch to see if they could pick up the spy's trail and had returned to Normanfenton.

Now he said, "But Normanfenton, how do we have any chance of stoppin' two divisions of Asafrics? There's only nine Boys left in the Bunch—"

"I said *you,* my boy, not your Bunch. What has to be done can be done by you alone, or it cannot be done at all."

The listener could have heard only that Normanfenton was going to send Dikar somewhere that must be kept a secret even from Marilee, and now there were soldiers in a little boat out on the lake to make sure no one climbed the ivy again.

"Why should anything be easier for me to do alone than with help?" Dikar asked.

"Please stop breaking in on me like that, young man." Normanfenton's tired smile took away the hurt of the sharp words. "Give me a chance to explain. One man can do what is to be done as well as nine or ninety.

"To get to where I am sending you, you will have to steal through the enemy's lines, through six hundred miles of territory held and patrolled by his troops. Capture will mean a particularly horrible death for you, for me the end of my last hope of checkmating Hashamoto.

"You will need every atom of your skill in moving silently and unseen, and any companion you take with you would only increase your peril."

"All right." Dikar shrugged. "Where am I goin', an' what am I to do there?"

Normanfenton turned back to the map. "You see how Mexico and then Central America narrow," his finger moved downward on the many-colored sheet pinned to the wall, "curving around the Gulf of Mexico to here, where the Panama Canal cuts through it."

"The Panama—That's where the tanks are comin' from!"

"That's where they will be coming from, according to the messages we've intercepted, about three or four weeks from now."

"Three or four weeks! What are they waitin' for?"

"DIVISIONS OF tanks cannot move at a moment's notice, my boy, like your Bunch. They've got to accumulate supplies of fuel, munitions, food, to sustain them on the march. Their machinery must be repaired, put in perfect order.

"There are innumerable details to be taken care of to prepare them for a long campaign, even more than usual for these divisions, which have been somewhat disorganized by their idleness. And all this, Dikar, must be done surreptitiously, lest the officers of vessels passing through the Canal observe the unusual activity and report it to the Asafric Supreme Command.

"Viceroy Hashamoto fears his own home government more than he does us," Normanfenton sighed. "And rightly."

"But if it's goin' to take 'em so long to get started an' we already know what they're up to, couldn't we get ready in that time to meet an' fight 'em?"

"Meet them where? They will have all Texas to spread out over, and we have no way of anticipating where they will choose to strike. Fight them how?

"In a battle of movement, tanks can be fought only by tanks, Dikar, and we have none. We have nothing that would give us the slightest chance against them unless—an' that's the whole crux of my plan—unless they can be taken by surprise, unprepared for action, their crews unsuspecting an enemy anywhere near.

"Now," the General went on, "all of this isthmus, except for some narrow stretches along its coast and along a few short, unconnected stretches of railway, remains pretty much the same as it was when Columbus first saw it.

"Where the Sierra Madre range does not thrust its crags to the sky, a thick and well-nigh impenetrable tropic growth bars travel. There is only one practicable route by which it can be traversed, the Pan-American Highway, a broad concrete road that was completed just a year before the invasion. Since Hashamoto does not dare requisition transports to convey his tanks by water, that is the way they must come."

Normanfenton's finger started moving back up on the map. "This way, Dikar, skirting the inward base of the mountains that join the Andes to the Rockies. Through Costa Rica, Nicaragua, Honduras.

"And here," the finger paused just before it would have crossed a line that zig-zagged across the picture of narrow land, the colors different each side of it, "as they approach Gautemala's Mexican border, is where they must be stopped, if they're to be stopped anywhere."

"Why there?" Dikar goggled. "Why just where the land's widest of all?" Beside where the general's finger rested a kind of bump stuck out into the water-blue. "I—I can't make out why you should pick that place."

"I'm picking it precisely because the land is widest here, because here the highway passes along the base of the Yucatan peninsula." Normanfenton pointed to the big bump. "Wilderness as the rest of the isthmus is, it is a tamed, gentle region compared to the primordial jungle of Yucatan. And, son, when the Asafric hordes overran Texas and Louisiana and Mississippi, a large number of Americans fled across the Gulf of Mexico to this green hell in Yucatan.

"Many of the boats that carried them were sunk by the guns of the enemy fleet. Many were wrecked by a hurricane. But some reached the shores of Yucatan and Campeche and Quintana Roo, and their passengers found sanctuary in the interior.

"What became of them we do not know. The sisal that was Yucatan's only crop was of no use to the Asafric, and so they did not bother to conquer that region. The underground wireless of the Secret Net never received a response from that green mystery. The jungle swallowed the refugees; they vanished."

DIKAR SCRATCHED his head. "You don't know how many there are. You don't know if they're still alive in there. You don't know anythin' about them. But you expect—"

"I know this about them," Normanfenton broke in. "I know that they were Americans once and that whatever they have become, whatever the jungle has done to them, if they still live they are still Americans.

"I'm gambling on that, Dikar. I'm gambling my hopes that the Cause I lead may still be saved, if you can reach them and tell them that their countrymen are fighting for freedom and are in danger."

"They'll come out of their jungles, when the Asafric tanks pass by—"

"And stop them." A thrill came into Normanfenton's deep voice, and as he turned to Dikar, he seemed suddenly taller in his faded, gray-blue uniform. "Stop them dead, there in the shadow of the Sierra Madre. Unless they do, we fail. I cannot believe God means to let us fail. I cannot believe that needing a miracle now, He will not help us work that miracle."

He spread wide his gnarled hands, bony and bulging with an old man's net of veins under yellowing, transparent skin. "I send you alone on a long, long road, Dikar, every inch of which will be fraught with peril of death for you.

"I send you into a steamy jungle to find men who for all I know may have turned into savages. I send you to ask them, for the sake of an ideal which almost surely they have forgotten, to attack trained soldiers who have conquered the world.

"By all the laws of reason it is a mad project, foredoomed to failure. I put my faith in that God who created men to be free, that it will succeed. And it must."

…Dikar walked slowly back across the top of Norrisdam. The hushed gray of dusk, sifting down through the tree-clad hills to veil the lake with darkling mist, was answered by a gray hush within him.

Dikar's eyes burned with long looking at the maps that

Normanfenton had showed him, hundreds of maps picturing every yard of the way he was to go. Dikar's head throbbed, full to bursting with all that Normanfenton had told him, with all the hundreds of things Dikar must not forget.

Dikar's heart ached with knowing that tonight, for the first time since he could remember, he must leave Marilee without telling her where he was going.

Tonight he was going to leave the Bunch that he'd been Boss of so long. Without a word of goodbye, he was going to slip away into the dark and he had as much hope of coming back to them as—as this twig, shooting over the dam's spillway and down into the foaming flood below, had of ever going back up the River to the woods.

Like that twig, Dikar was being carried along by a rushing river, far and far from the woods he'd loved, far from the Mountain that was his home.

TO DIKAR'S left and right, along the sides of the clearing into which he'd come were the little houses that Walt had called log-cabins when he'd brought the Bunch here to show them where they were to live. At the other end a great fire sent its leaping, orange light up into the spreading branches of a tall oak.

Down the middle of the open space a long table ran, the Girls bustling around it as they set it for supper. The firelight danced on the Girls' smooth, brown arms, on the thighs peeping briefly through the lustrous cloaks of their hair. Almost as tall as Dikar, but black-haired and bearded, Johnstone talked with Alfoster. Nearer the fire, Patmara and Abestein and Henfield threw little stones at a mark they had blazed on the oak.

The clearing was filled with happy laughter, friendly chatter, but beyond the fire the woods were black and the sunset wind made a rushing sound in the treetops.

"Dikar!"

Marilee had seen him. She was coming toward him, her hands held out to him, her body slim and straight. Every graceful line of her, every movement was a song swelling in Dikar's throat, an ache in his arms.

As Dikar waited for Marilee, the fire flared and he saw another girl who stood very still in the shadows. Her form was slim and straight as Marilee's, but the long fall of hair that robed it was a lusterless black. Her eyes seemed to watch Marilee, but there was no life in them. Her hands hung empty, half open as though something very dear had spilled from them and was gone forever.

Bessalton.

The wind in the treetops made a rushing sound, like that of a wide, dark river flowing from here into the far and lonely night.

CHAPTER 8
NO FAREWELL

IT WAS very dark in the cabin, so dark that Dikar could not see Marilee at all, though he could feel her warm, soft body close against his; smell the clean, fresh sweetness of her; hear the whisper of her long, tired breathing that told him she was deep in sleep at last.

He'd waited a long time, staring aching-eyed into the dark, till he could be certain that she slept. Now, very carefully, he slid his arm from under her and slipped from the bed, and she did not stir.

Dikar's heart was very heavy, but his feet were light and silent as he felt for and found the apron of twigs Marilee had plaited for him on their Mountain. He tied it around him, fastened to its belt his knife in the sheath Marilee had made for him out of the skin of a deer. These were the only things Dikar took with him from the cabin. These—and the memory of Marilee.

Dikar saw nothing of the dark woods as he went down through them. He heard nothing of the uncountable little voices

of the woods. He went down through them silent as any creature that prowls the sunless hours, but only because he could
not move through the woods in any other way, not because he
gave thought to what he was doing.

He'd shut out thought, because if he thought what he was
doing, he could not do it at all.

A sound of voices stopped him, at the bottom of the wooded
hill.

Dikar crouched just within the bushes that ended the woods,
peered out at the road that crossed the top of Norrisdam and
then went around this hill and away. The voices came from the
black hulk of a big, covered truck that loomed out there against
the lake's paler glimmer.

Dikar rounded his mouth and made the sound of a hoot-owl.

"WHAT'S THE idea startin' us out this time uh night," one of
the voices grumbled, "without us even knowin' what we're carryin'
or where we're goin'?"

Dikar could see other trucks standing on the road. There
were five of them, and this was the middle one. "You think
they're gonna tell you?" another hoarse voice said. "Yer in the
army now, Carson. Yer not behin' th' plow."

"Plow, hell! I was runnin' a loom over to Sweetwater before
I joined up. With a big Black crackin' a bull-whip across my
back every time a thread got snarled. First thing I did, when I
heard our boys come a-whoopin' inter town, I grabbed thet
whip out of his han' an' spattered his brains all over the floor
with its butt."

"What're yeh crabbin' about, then?"

"Who's crabbin'? Cripes! Fer what Fenton done fer me, he
could tell me t'go jump off th' top uh thet dam there an' I'd do
it. All I'm sayin', I'm hankerin' to know what's the idea us bein'
turned out in th' dead uh night an' findin' these trucks a-waitin'
fer us, all loaded an' locked up so's we don't know whut's in 'em.

"Why? I'll tell yeh why, Tom Carson. Thar's spies in camp.
That's why."

"Spies, me eye! Thet's a lot uh bunk."

"The hell it is. Didn't one get away this mornin', thet climbed up th' wall uh Headquarters ter take a shot at General Fenton?"

"I still say it's bunk, if that bunch uh Dikar's couldn't even spot where the guy come out o' th' lake, there wasn't never no guy in it. They even sent divers down t' see if he was caught in th' spillway an' they couldn't—"

"All right, men!" The dark shape that was suddenly in the road had Walt's voice. "You'll be moving in a minute. Your instructions remain unchanged. Maintain as much distance behind the truck ahead as you can without losing sight of it. Watch for a sudden stop. Show no lights, keep your motor running as quietly as possible, and on no account use your horn. Is that perfectly clear?"

"Yes, Cap'n Bennet."

"I shall be on the leading truck. In case of emergency, cut your muffler out for a count of two and I'll stop the motorcade, come back to you. That's all."

Walt moved on toward the head of the line. Carson exclaimed softly. "Must be somethin' big up ef th' general's own pussonal aide's ridin' with us."

Dikar's muscles were twitching under his skin. He was really going. When Walt had said, "Your instructions remain un-changed," he'd told Dikar that Normanfenton had heard nothing new to make him change his mind. When Walt had said, "I shall be on the leading truck," he'd told Dikar that he was going along as far as the trucks were going.

THE MOTOR of the first truck made sound. Another one throbbed in the darkness, and now the one here in front of Dikar came alive. It was moving. The next one came slowly past him, and then the last.

Dikar lifted out in the road, leaped for the narrow shelf across its back. His foot missed, his fingerhold on a knob at the corner slipped; and then his toes caught in a loop of chain and he was all right.

The truck was moving very slowly. Dikar got up on the little shelf, groped for the padlock that held the doors closed. A tug, and it came loose. Dikar pulled one door open, climbed in through it, pulled it shut, making sure it didn't slam. The blackness was thick, but his hand found a loose little board at the door's edge, and he turned it to hold the door closed.

The hoot-owl signal to Walt, the padlock that wasn't really locked, this little board, were the first three of all the things Normanfenton had given Dikar to remember.

He was squeezed between the door and what felt like a rough wooden wall rising just inside. The truck swayed a lot. That was because the road twisted like a snake, crawling down the hillside. Wheels rumbled underneath and the chain that had saved Dikar clanked as it hit up against something.

The clanking stopped, all of a sudden, just as there was a soft bump against the end of the truck. Dikar's scalp prickled, and then he remembered how narrow the road down the hill was, so narrow that the bushes on either side of it would scrape the sides of the trucks.

In some places the boughs of trees met over the road. It must be a very leafy bough hanging low that had bumped the truck's roof.

Now they must be at the bottom of the hill and the road must be getting straight, because the rumbling told Dikar they were going faster and faster. He squeezed around to face the wooden wall and his hands crawled up it, feeling that it was made up of big wooden boxes, piled high. When he got his arms stretched up over his head, he could just reach the top of the boxes. His hands closed on an edge and he pulled himself up.

The space under the truck's roof was just big enough for Dikar to scrouge into it. He didn't have to inch along very far before the top of the boxes ended.

Dikar worked himself around till he lay sidewise along the

inner edge of the boxes and then let his legs down over the edge. He dropped down into a black space.

THE SPACE was as wide as the truck, but toward the front another wall of boxes closed it off. Just the other side of this there must be a hole in the front wall of the truck because Dikar could hear someone say, "I don't see why they're makin' us drive in the dark. It would be different if we weren't allowed to show as many lights and fires as we want around camp."

"We ain't in camp, now, you dope. The Asafrics ain't sendin' planes to bomb us there 'cause they don't want to wreck the dam, but we're gettin' far enough away from it so they don't have to be afraid of that. If they spot us now...."

Dikar didn't pay any more attention to what the men up front were saying. He was down on his knees and his fingers were prying at the side of the middle box of the lowest row.

It swung out like a door. Dikar reached inside the box, found a round thing that was cold to the feel. He touched a little knob on its side, and light leaped out from it.

The light showed him other things in the box. There was a green uniform spotted with the dried blood of the dead Asafric it had belonged to. There was a shiny revolver and a shiny leather belt filled with bullets.

There were two of the flat glasses that you could look into and see yourself in, even better than you could see yourself in a clear, smooth pool in the woods. Dikar remembered their name. Mirrors. Dikar grinned, thinking how excited Marilee got the first time she'd seen one. He mustn't think about Marilee! Not yet. Not till it didn't hurt so much to think about her.

Beside the mirrors, there were a comb and a bottle of the black water Walt had used to make Dikar's hair and beard black, that time last fall when Dikar kidnaped Major Benjamin Apgar, the American spy who for years had been on Hashamoto's staff.

Dikar hung the flashlight on a nail sticking out from the side of the truck. He fixed the mirrors, one on each wall of boxes, so that he could see the face and back of his head. Picking up the comb and the bottle of black water, he went to work on his hair and beard.

All the time he worked, the rumble of wheels went on underneath him, carrying him on into the night.

When he'd finished the job as well as he could, Dikar started to put on the green uniform. His legs got all tangled up in it, and he was thrown down as the truck went around a curve and bumped his head, but he got it fixed right at last.

He was glad they'd found out that a lot of the Abyssinians didn't wear shoes, because the uniform only made him feel uncomfortable and clumsy but with shoes on he would have been good for nothing.

Dikar fastened the belt around his waist and put the revolver into the pocket fixed on the belt to hold it. There was another pocket on the belt for a knife. Dikar put his own knife into it.

He bent and put into the box the limp sheath that Marilee had made for his knife, and the apron of plaited twigs that he'd brought from the Mountain. Lifting, Dikar saw in the mirror a tall, swart Abyssinian in Asafric green, black-bearded and scowling.

Underneath him the wheels rumbled, rolling faster and faster.

Dikar put the other things away into the box, the flashlight last. The dark that came when he thumbed the little button on its side seemed even blacker than before. He closed the side of the box, settled down on the floor, his back propped against the box on the other side.

He was very tired. He was so tired that the rolling rumble of the wheels blurred, was like the rush of a wide, dark river....

A loud snort woke him. The truck had stopped.

"What's up?" The soldier up front was frightened. "Cripes, Jordan, what's stopped us?"

CHAPTER 9

I'LL RIDE THE RIVER

"WHY—WHY'D YOU signal Cap Bennet?" the scared soldier babbled. "I don't see nothin'." Dikar could imagine him, staring wide-eyed into the dark, his hands tight on his gun. "I don't see nobody."

"Relax," the other man up there said. "There ain't nothin' to see. We're stopped because we're fresh out of gas, that's all."

"Out? You're nuts," the first one yelped. "I checked the gauge when we started an' it said—"

"Full tank. Sure. It says the same thing now an' we been running damn near all night. That gauge is jammed, Cal, an' the monkey was supposed to fill us up must of went by it."

Cal groaned. "What do we do now?"

"Ask the captain. Here he comes."

Dikar pushed himself to his feet, made sure the revolver and his knife were safe in the belt. Walt's voice came in to him, low but plain. "What's the trouble, men?"

Both talked at once, telling him.

"That's rank carelessness." Walt sounded awful mad. "Somebody will be sorry for it when I get back. But we can't hold up the whole convoy; I've got to get it to Cairo before daylight."

"Hey, Cap. How's about we siphon some gas out of each of the other tanks?"

"Mmmmm. No. It would take too long. Besides, they all might run out, if we do that. I guess we'll have to leave you— Oh damn! You men are supposed to go on to Betteville first thing in the morning. All right!" he snapped, as if he'd just made up his mind. "Here's how we'll work it.

"You two men go up to the lead truck and tell Sergeant Carnorvan I want him to take the other four trucks on to Cairo, and then find places in them for yourselves. I'll stay here and guard this one till you can send some gas back here to me. Get going!"

"Yes sir." Scraping noises from up front told Dikar that Jordan and the other soldier were getting off. He reached up, chinned himself to the top of the boxes. The space under the roof was a tight fit, on account of the uniform he had on now, but he managed to crawl through to the back end and squeeze down again to the floor.

A throb of motors beat against the truck. Faded. Gravel crunched outside, and knuckles thumped on the truck-door. Dikar twisted away the little board that held the door closed.

FRESH AIR was like a drink of cold water after the thick, stinking stuff he'd been breathing. There was still no moon but Walt's head and shoulders were plain against the paler dark.

Dikar dropped down alongside of him and said, "You did that good. The way you talked, those soldiers couldn't ever guess it was you that fixed things so they'd have to stop here."

"Yes," Walt chuckled, "the whole thing worked out swell. You've disappeared from camp and no one can possibly know which way you went, or how."

Dikar thought of something. "Hey! Won't the men who unload the truck wonder why the boxes are piled that way, with a big hole in the middle?"

"Nobody's going to unload it. I'm going to set it afire, and report that it was done by an Asafric patrol from whom I escaped by the skin of my teeth."

Dikar stiffened. "That's what Cal was scared of! The Blacks do prowl around here."

"Right enough. We're quite near their outposts here and every now and then some of them slip through our lines to do as much damage as they can, under cover of night.

"But the way you look, you'll have to worry more about being spotted by our friends rather than by the enemy. Which is why we'd better quit wasting time gabbing. Come on. I'll show you just where we are, so you can make what distance you can before daylight. This way,"

They went around the end of the truck and abruptly Dikar stopped, pulling back against Walt's hand on his arm. "Wait!"

"Yes. We're in a town."

"But the noise the trucks made sure must have waked someone up. They'll see us."

"The trucks didn't wake anyone up, Dikar," Walt spoke in a queer, flat tone. "Take another look."

Dikar's eyes narrowed.

The houses didn't just look black because they stood against the sky. They were black, the black of charred wood. Not one of them had glass in its windows, or a whole roof.

Over here there were just two walls standing to make a corner. That gap, down there, wasn't a big garden but a tumbled heap of burned timbers. The high thing sticking up out of it was a chimney standing guard over the ashes of a home.

"No, Dikar. Our trucks couldn't make a loud enough noise to wake the people who sleep in those houses. They are the most fortunate of those who once lived here. The others—" Walt shrugged. "It's the old story. It's happened thousands of times in the last twelve years, all over America. Someone's capacity for endurance came to an end and he turned on his tormentor. His neighbors paid for his crime.... Come on over here. I want to show you something."

Dikar, stumbling along beside him, was too heartsick with thinking of what had happened here to watch or care where he was being led. "Look down there," Walt said, stopping him and pointing.

THE HOUSES were just black sticks, leaping every which way, so you could look right through them. Looking through them, Dikar saw water, glinting faintly in the dark. The water was so wide Dikar could not see the land on its other side. It was a wide, dark river.

Dikar struck savagely at the Asafric officer.

"The Mississippi," Walt said, "on its way to the Gulf of Mexico. Its flow will give you your direction."

"You've got a boat to take me down it, like the one you had to take me down the Hudson to New York, that time. I—"

"No, Dikar!" Walt broke in. "That would be sheer suicide. Maybe you could get down almost to Memphis without discovery—there's enough of the night left—but the Asafrics hold that city and all the territory below it.

"From there on down the river is crowded with their vessels, gunboats, freighters, all kinds of boats moving troops to and from garrisons, batches of slaves to the various plantations. You couldn't travel a hundred yards without being seen, and you have five hundred miles to go."

"Five hundred!" Muscles knotted under the skin of Dikar's face. "It would take me weeks on foot, Walt." His fingers dug into Walt's arm. "I'm goin' down that river. I don't know how, but I've got to go down it to get to Yucatan in time, and so I'll find a way."

"By Jove," his friend said, softly. "I've got a hunch you will.

I've heard your voice sound like that before. More power to you, Dikar." He tried to pull away, and in the dark Dikar could just make out his twisted grin. "Good luck, boy."

"Wait, Walt." Dikar held on. "Listen. There's somethin I want you to do for me when you get back to Norrisdam. I—I couldn't lie to Marilee. I couldn't tell her I was just goin' away for a little while so—so I didn't tell her anythin' at all. Will you go and tell her that I—that I've gone away from her, far an' far, an' that I'm not ever comin' back. Will you, Walt?"

"No. I won't tell Marilee that you're not coming back. I don't even want to think of it myself. You are coming back, Dikar."

"Maybe I am. Maybe a long, long time from now, when we've chased the Asafrics out of America I'll come back to Marilee. But I can't till then, an' I don't want her waitin' and waitin' for me.

"I want her to be mad at me, so mad that she'll stop lovin' me. The first hurt will be worse that way, but it will be over quicker, an' then Marilee will forget me an'—and find herself another mate."

When Walt spoke, his voice was low, and kind of shaky. "I guess you're right. I guess— All right, I'll tell her." He rubbed his hand down his leg, stuck it out at Dikar.

Dikar took Walt's hand and squeezed, and then Walt was going back to the truck and Dikar was going toward the River, through the tumbled jungle of the burned houses.

The blackened timbers were almost as thick as the trees of the woods, but they did not smell like the trees. They must have burned a long time ago, but the smell of their burning stuck to them, and there was a smell of something else that had burned— not wood, but flesh.

Dikar stopped all of a sudden, the blackened timbers blotting out any sight of sky or road, the rough wood hurting his feet. He stood rigid, his lip curling, a prickle running up and down his back.

Dikar couldn't see anything. He couldn't hear anything, but he knew there were eyes on him, somewhere in this dark.

Dikar's hand went to the butt of his gun, closed on it. Someone hidden in these black, gaunt ruins was looking at him.

There was a sudden swoosh, behind him, and a burst of leaping light. Walt had fired the truck. Out from between two black timbers a wild shape leaped at Dikar, knife gleaming as it sliced down at him. Dikar brought up his gun to shoot—

From behind, cold fingers clamped his wrist, jerked the revolver sidewise.

CHAPTER 10

THE NIGHT KNIFE

JERKED OFF-BALANCE, Dikar went down into the welter of burned junk. The knife missed him clean as the first Asafric lurched past and vanished in a crash of charred wood. But the other one hung on, falling on top of him.

For moments they struggled silently, their breath harsh and broken. But all Dikar's great strength could not throw off the heavy, powerful body of the Asafric. Dikar was pinned down, writhing; and now he felt a hand slide to his throat and tighten there. Frantically he twisted, but the hand clenched tighter and his strength was ebbing fast.

Then Dikar felt the Asafric's body jerk spasmodically; the next instant it had gone lax. With a last effort Dikar heaved it from him, and he struggled to his feet, gasping.

He swayed there—staring into the frightened white face of Marilee. Her hand still held a bloody knife.

"Marilee! How—"

With a little sob she dropped the knife and ran to him. "First I thought you were an Asafric," she whispered against his chest. "Then I saw your eyes and I knew. And then I—I killed him."

He held her fiercely. "But how'd you get here, Marilee?"

"On top of the truck you were in."

"On top—" Dikar remembered the bump on the roof. "You followed me—" Suddenly he thrust her from him and down, so that she was crouched on the ground. "Stay down, Marilee. The other one is hidin' over there."

The flames from the burning truck were dying now, and all around him the weird shadows were moving, like naked Blacks creeping from every side. "Why did you follow me, Marilee?"

"Because you were mis'rable, an' I had to know why."

"I was what?"

"Heartsick, Dikar. I've lived with you too long not to read it on your face when you came back from Headquarters. All through supper I knew it, an' after, in our cabin, I waited for you to tell me about it. But you didn't.

"Oh Dikar," a sob caught in Marilee's throat, and Dikar's arms ached with wanting to take her in them again and comfort her. "You'd shut me away from you. There was something between us, cold an' dark an'—an' terrible." He didn't dare even look at her. If he took his eyes off the shadows, that would be the killer's chance to jump them.

"I knew you weren't asleep," Marilee went on. "I knew you were only waitin' for me to fall asleep, so that you could do somethin' you didn't want me to know about, somethin' that made you sick even to think about doin'. I had to know what it was. I just had to. So I made believe to fall asleep—"

"You fooled me, all right."

"Then you got up and started down the hill an' I trailed you in the treetops, keeping far behind, by the sounds you made. That wasn't like you, Dikar, to make any sounds at all goin' through the woods, an' it made me even more worried. Then you crossed a clearin' an' I saw you. You were—funny. Like you were walkin' in your sleep."

"That's the way I felt, Marilee." The truck was almost burnt out. Pretty soon it would be black dark. "Like I was walkin' in a nightmare."

THIS WAS like a nightmare too, the black ruins all about, the dying firelight, the shivery feel of death waiting somewhere in the deepening shadows. No sound but Marilee's low words.

"While you crouched there at the side of the road, I watched you from a treetop down near the last truck. When the trucks started movin', I saw you jump on the back of the last one an' climb in, and then, Dikar, I saw another dark figure dart out of the woods, jump on the back of that same truck and hang there!"

"Hang? On the chain! That's why it stopped clankin! Someone else trailed me—the spy, of course. The spy that got away this afternoon!"

"The trucks had gone around a curve so there was no use my yellin', but I cut across, still in the treetops, to where the road curves around the hill, got there in time to drop down on top of the one you were in."

"I thought that was a low branch hittin' the roof."

"I was just goin to yell down to its drivers when I remembered that the spy would hear me an' get away. So I just stayed up there—"

"An' rode like that all night. Oh Marilee! Suppose you'd fallen off?"

"I almost did," she said, simply, "lots of times. It was slippery up there an' the cold wind pulled at me. Well, anyways, when the truck stopped, the spy dropped off an' dived in among those burned buildins here so fast that all I could see was a flittin' shadow. Then Walt was down there under me.

"While he was talkin' to the soldiers, I let myself down on the other side of the truck and crawled along in a ditch a ways, an' then went across the road fast to the side where the spy was".

"Why in thunder did you do that?"

"I wanted to see who the spy was."

"What for?" The last light flickered out and the dreadful dark closed in. "What difference does it make who he is?" Dikar's body hummed like a stretched bowstring.

"What difference? Look, Dikar. He'd trailed you through the woods without either you or me hearin' him. Who else could have done that except—"

"No," Dikar groaned, her meaning terribly clear to him. "It couldn't be a—"

"Look out!" Marilee half-screamed. *"Behind!"* Dikar whirled to a sudden black shape, his gun whipping up.

"Don't shoot," the shape said, quietly. "Don't shoot me, Dikar."

"Bessalton!" Marilee exclaimed. It's Bessalton, Dikar, not the spy."

"YES, MARILEE." Bessalton's voice was flat and tired. "The spy. I swam to the Headquarters wall from where the Bunch was in swimmin' an' I swam back to you, under water, when I fell from the wall, an' nobody noticed that I hadn't been with you all the time."

"You were the spy— Why, Bessalton?" Marilee was standing now. "Why did you spy on Dikar, an' follow him?"

"That's clear enough," Dikar said grimly. "She figures that we killed Franksmith, so she's turned Mudskin to get even."

"Mudskin! Me! How can you say such a thing?" Bessalton blazed back.

"I can say it all right." Dikar's throat was tight with his anger, "because it is so. Why else did you spy on us?"

"I had to, Dikar. I had to find out what Normanfenton wanted. I'd sent Franksmith to die on Clingman's Dome, an' the others who're buried up there, an' now there were only nine of you Boys left. I wasn't goin' to let Normanfenton send you to die too. I was goin' to stop him somehow.

"An' then I saw Normanfenton's face as he said America is in danger, an' I heard his voice as he told you that you were the only one who could save America, an' I knew that I couldn't stop you from goin' where he was sendin' you. But I could go along, without your knowin' it, an' maybe I could save you from gettin' killed—"

"Get killed yourself, is more like it."

"Maybe get killed myself," Bessalton agreed, "an' go to Frank-smith. He's waitin' for me, Dikar, somewhere out there in the dark. I've heard him callin' me." All of a sudden her low voice was edged by a strange, spine-chilling shrillness. "Every night I hear him callin' me—"

"That's crazy," Dikar exclaimed. "He's dead, Bessalton, an'—"

"No, Dikar," Marilee broke in. "It's not crazy. I'd feel the same way if you went away from me an' never came back. I'd hear your voice callin' me.

"When a Girl gives a Boy her love, there is no life for her any more except as part of his life. If he shuts her out from it, he kills her just as sure as if he stuck a knife in her heart, only more cruelly."

That was what Dikar was doing. He was shutting Marilee out from his life—she knew it. That was why she had said this. "Wait." He had to gain time to think this out. "Bessalton, did you see the Asafric that jumped at me with the knife? Where'd he go?"

"I tried to follow him, Dikar, soon as I knew you weren't an Asafric. But I couldn't find him." She shivered. "I was goin' to try to kill him."

"Dikar," Marilee said, "why are you dressed up like an Asafric? What are you goin' to do?"

He stared at her, feeling a sudden, new anguish. Here it was, the question he'd sneaked out of the cabin to keep from having her ask. "I can't tell you, Marilee," he said at length. That was the answer she'd just told him would be like his sticking a knife into her. "Normanfenton ordered me not to, an' Normanfenton's our Boss an' I've got to obey him."

"You—can't—tell—me." Dikar strained to see Marilee's face in the dark, but all he could see was that she stood straight in the dimness. "What right has Normanfenton to order you to shut me out from you?"

"Every right," he answered, miserably. "His plan to checkmate Hashamoto's move to smash our whole cause won't work if a hint of it leaks out. Oh, Marilee. I'm sorry. I'm dreadful sorry, but I can't tell anyone, not even you—"

"You are mistaken." A soft, lisping voice said behind Dikar. "Don't move!" All of a sudden black, burly shapes blotted the darkness behind the girls, and lifted knives struck blue sparks out of the darkness. "If you move, American, your women die."

CHAPTER 11
DOWN THE DARK RIVER

THE RIVER was a dark rush through the night and Dikar was being carried along on the breast of its black flood. His ankles were tied, his wrists tied behind his back so tight that his brow was wet with sweat, and he could barely hear the soft, silken murmur of the question that was being asked him for the twentieth time.

"What is Fenton's plan?"

The Asafrics had tied up Marilee and Bessalton and laid them in the bottom of the little boat, but they'd made Dikar sit between them so that the officer could ask him, again and again:

"What is Fenton's plan, American?"

Dikar kept his lips tight shut, but his eyes looked hate at the man who faced him, from the board across the middle of the boat under which the Girls' legs had been shoved.

"You are not very wise," murmured Lieutenant Yosuke, "to be so stubborn." Dikar knew his name because one of the Blacks had called him that while they were taking their prisoners down to the ruined pier under which they'd hidden this boat.

"If I can report to my commander that I have obtained the whole story, I shall win a promotion. For that," he lifted the gun he held in his lap, "I am willing to pay you with the mercy of a clean death."

The sky was faintly paling with the false dawn and against it, in the very front of the boat, Dikar could see the crouched, motionless bulk of a Black who silently watched the dark bank. The sky's grayness lay on the water, out further, but the other Black, bent over an oar in the back of the boat, kept it in the shadow of the bank.

"What is Fenton's plan, American?" Yosuke had told Dikar that the glare of flames from the truck had been seen by the Asafrics as they returned from a scout further up the river. They'd come in to shore and two men had been sent to investigate. One of them had returned to report to Yosuke after discovering that Dikar was not alone.

"You would be very wise," Yosuke's silken, patient voice murmured, "to tell Fenton's plan to me now. If you wait till we get to Memphis, you will beg to tell it to anyone who will listen."

Dikar said slowly, "Nothing you can do will make me talk."

"No?" Yosuke sighed. "I imagine not. Nothing we can do to you—you Americans are very stubborn about such things as duty and honor. That is why I have burdened myself with these two women, instead of having them killed back there."

Dikar felt the muscles knot along the edge of his jaw. "What do you mean?" he asked hoarsely.

Yosuke smiled. "The Blacks," he said. "The Blacks will have charge of the women. You would not like that."

"You dog!" Dikar spat at him. "You filthy, yellow dog!"

"You dare to call me—" Yosuke lashed out to slice the sight of his gun across Dikar's face. Dikar's right hand flashed from behind his back, grabbed the revolver; his left fist cracked against the Yellow officer's jaw. Yosuke sagged down.

Lifting Yosuke's gun, Dikar pounded bullets into the Asafric up front, pounded him over into the river. Dikar laughed triumphantly, twisted to the man behind him. The Black had dropped his oar and was snatching up a rifle. His tied legs cramped between the Girls', Dikar couldn't get his arm around far enough to aim at the Black.

The rifle swept up to point straight at his head, shattered the silence with its roar, the darkness with its lightning. But in that split-second Dikar had thrown himself sideways over the boat's side and he was going down into the lightless rush of the river.

ITS COLD struck into him like a thousand knives, numbed him. The weight of the water in his clothes dragged him down into the black depths. He could not kick free from the bonds on his ankles, no matter how frantically he struggled. He was sinking—drowning.

Held air tore at Dikar's lungs, his mind was blurred now. His feet struck the River's bed and kicked, and he was going up again.

His head broke water. Breath burst from him in a great gasp. A scream drew his gaze to the boat, beyond reach, and he saw the Black, gigantic, standing, rifle lifted, butt down, to smash it where the Girls' heads must be.

Dikar brought knees up into his belly, straightened them with a frantic strength that shot him half out of water and to the boat. His hands clamped on the Asafric's straddled legs, his shoulders heaved. A flailing dark form sailed over his head, sent up a tremendous splash.

The splash blinded Dikar and then cleared away. A black log came up in the whitish foam-boil, rolled, and was moving shoreward. It was the Black. If he got to land, he'd spread the alarm and Dikar's journey would be ended before it had hardly started.

Dikar couldn't stop him. He'd lost his gun and he didn't dare let go the boat. Suddenly something struck him—the oar. He grabbed it, pointed its handle end at the swimming Asafric, threw it with all the power he could.

Not for nothing had he killed deer with spears, on the Mountain. The heavy oar flew straight to its mark. There was a crack, a flurry of arms and legs and foam.

There was nothing but foam out there on the top of the rushing waters. Foam and the bobbing oar.

The boat rocked, with someone moving inside. Who? The scream he'd heard had been Bessalton's. Had the Black smashed his rifle-butt down once already? Was Marilee— Her name burst from Dikar in a great sob as he twisted, got his other hand on the boat's edge, fought to pull himself up. "Marilee!"

"Dikar!"

He could breathe again as he looked down and saw two pale ovals in the black bottom of the boat. "Dikar," Marilee gasped. "Are you all right?"

"Fine." He ached all over, would have to rest before he could drag himself up and over, but he wasn't lying. "I'm fine an' that Black won't bother us any more." He strained to see what was in the middle of the boat. "How about the lieut'nant?"

"He hasn't stirred since you hit him. Oh, Dikar! That was wonderful, the way you called him a name to bring him close enough for you to get at him."

"What was wonderful was the way you gnawed through my cords, behind my back. How did you ever think of that?"

"How could I help thinkin' of it, with your hands right down on my chin? But I had to scrouge down to get my teeth to them, an' if Yosuke had noticed—"

"He was too busy with me to notice anything. What had me shivering, though, was the fellow right back of you. If he'd seen—"

"He couldn't. It was so dark down here I couldn't see your wrists myself, just felt them. I guess you can make me out now because the sky is getting lighter. It must be near sunrise."

"I guess—" Dikar, looking up, checked. "That isn't sunrise, Marilee!" The dim glow that had come into the sky had a reddish, scary shade. "The sun doesn't come up in the south."

"What then?" Marilee was startled. "A fire?"

"No. It's the lights of Memphis! We must be gettin' close. We'll be seen, as soon as the River carries us past that point of land. I've got to stop this boat!"

"How?"

"If I hold on an' kick, maybe I can swing it in enough to hit the point instead of passin' it. Like this…."

THE THICKET of bushes and weeds and tall grass was still more gray than green in the clouded dawn as Dikar lifted from making sure that Lieutenant Yosuke had not loosened the vines with which he was tied up, or worked the gag of leaves out of his mouth.

Marilee and Bessalton pushed through the screen of leaves from beyond which there came the rushing sound of the river waters.

"All right?" Dikar asked, low-toned. "All right," Marilee answered. "We found where a willow makes a curtain of its branches, dipping down into the water, and hid the boat behind it. What did you find out on your scout?"

"There's a road back there." Dikar pointed. "But from the looks of things no one ever stops here." There was no need for him to tell about the bunch of ivy he'd seen swaying from a tall pole beside the road, a yellow skull grinning out at him from its heart. "This ground around here was once cleared, but it's all overgrown like this, deserted and desolate. Down the road a little is a big house, but no sign that anyone's lived in it for years. We seem to be pretty safe here, till we're ready to leave."

"That's good. We all need rest." Marilee's eyes went to Yosuke. "One of us will have to keep watchin' him, though, Dikar."

"Why?" Bessalton was looking at the Asafric officer too, her nostrils pinched, queer whitish lines around her mouth, her fingers touching the hilt of the knife she carried in a fold of her sarong.

"Why can't we do what he would, just slice his throat an' be done with him? If he'd died like his two men died, you wouldn't be worryin' about him, would you?"

"If he'd died in fair fight," Dikar explained, "it would have been fine, but we can't just kill him when he hasn't a chance to defend himself."

"Why?" Bessalton asked again.

"Because we can't. It's the code." Dikar made a little brushing motion with his hand. "Never mind. I'll figure out later what to do with him. What we've got to figure out now is how you Girls are goin to get back to Norrisdam."

"Wrong," Marilee said. "We haven't got to figure that out, because Bessalton and I have decided we're not goin' back. We're goin' with you."

"YOU DECIDED!" Dikar didn't know whether to laugh or be mad. "I suppose the President's orders that I am to go alone have nothin' to do with it."

"They have not," she snapped back. "Normanfenton may be President an' the smartest man in America, but he's not a—an angel. He can make mistakes and this is one time he's made one. Suppose you'd been alone last night, Dikar. Where would you be now?"

Dikar knew it was no use arguing with her. He'd learned long ago that when Marilee said something with her little chin stuck out like that and her small fists curled at her sides, you couldn't change her, but he'd never learned not to try.

"Look, honey. I—" He couldn't just lay down the law to her, he couldn't send her away without her understanding why. "Look. Let's go off where that Asafric can't hear, an' I'll explain why I can't take you with me." He put his hand on her arm and they moved off, and only afterward Dikar realized that they'd forgotten all about Bessalton.

Leaves rustled against them, thorns plucked at them. Marilee stopped. "This is far enough, Dikar. Go ahead."

"You mustn't repeat a word of this, even in your sleep."

"Do you have to tell me that?"

"No. Well, Marilee, here's the story." He told her about it, in as few words as he could. "So you see," he ended, "why Normanfenton said that I must go alone."

"Yes. I see why he said it, an' I still think he is wrong. Look, Dikar. If you go alone, an' you're captured or killed, that's the end of everything. But if the three of us try to get through to this Yucatan, there's three chances of one of us gettin' there. The chances might be more against each one of the three, but the chances against America would be less."

Dikar rubbed the back of his head with his knuckles. "I—I guess I'm dumb. When I listened to Normanfenton he seemed right. Now you seem right. But you can't both be."

"No, we can't both be." She moved a little away. "It's up to you, Dikar." Her gray eyes took hold of his. "It's all up to you."

"Up to me? If I say so, you'll stop arguin' an' go back to Norrisdam?"

"If you say that you must go alone, I will not try to go with you."

She always twisted his words around. The light wind that stirred the leaves was suddenly cold on Dikar's skin. Marilee stood straight and proud in the dimness and something in the way her eyes rested on him reminded Dikar of what she'd said last night: "When a Girl gives a Boy her love—there is no life for her any more except as a part of his life."

A bird cheeped its joy at finding a worm. Underlying the tiny morning sounds in the brush was the sound of the wide river rushing endlessly to the Gulf.

Dikar couldn't think with Marilee's eyes on him. He looked away from Marilee. Through an opening in the shimmering green, he saw a piece of the river. He saw a broken plank, caught in the grasp of the swift current, shoot across the space of muddy water and vanish downstream.

"HELP ME, Marilee," Dikar murmured. "You've always helped me to find the right thing to do." He looked at Marilee. Her hand was pressed against her breast, as if something hurt her. "Help me this once more."

"No." The hand pressed harder against the soft round of her breast. "This is a thing I cannot help you with. It is a thing for you to decide yourself."

Dikar couldn't bear looking at that hand, knowing that the hurt under it was on account of him. He looked at the river again. Two branches, held together by their intertwined twigs came into view. A swirl of the current brought them to the inner edge of the water. Something on the shore caught one of them, held it. The current tore the other one away, slanted it out toward the middle of the river. The twisted little twigs of the one left behind quivered as if reaching after the branch that had come so far with it.

There was no use of it reaching. The river had separated them. The river would never let them come together again. Anything caught in the rush of the river must obey the will of the river.

"No, Marilee," Dikar said, still not looking at her. "It is nothing for me to decide. It is something that has been decided for me. I have my orders an—Wait!"

Out there in the river something black, small, had appeared. A muskrat's head. A long, V-shaped ripple trailed behind it, and the V slanted toward the shore across the streaks of foam that marked the current that had swept the branch out away from it.

The strength of the muskrat was so small, so awfully small against the strength of the river, but the muskrat wanted to get to shore, and it was setting its will against the will of the river.

A spray of leaves hid it from Dikar, but it was much nearer the shore than when he'd first glimpsed it. He swung around to Marilee and his words came swiftly. "What I have to do, I've got to do," he cried. "But I'm a man, not a stick of wood, so I'll do it my own way. You're goin with me, my Marilee."

"Dikar!" A light that had almost gone out flared again and shone brilliant in the gray eyes. "Oh Dikar—"

A loud threshing of brush broke in on her, the pound of running feet. Dikar whirled, threw himself toward it. Something thudded to the ground, just beyond a bush that blocked his view. He got around the bush and stopped, his eyes widening.

Bessalton stood rigid, the blade of the knife in her hand scarlet, looking down at Yosuke who sprawled at her feet, face down and very still.

MARILEE CAME up, gasped, stopped close to Dikar. Bessalton's head turned to them. "He must have rubbed the vines around his feet against a stone," she said, "till he rubbed them through. First thing I knew, he'd jumped up an' started to run. I caught up with him and—and—well, there wasn't anything else I could do, was there?"

"No," Marilee said, flat-toned. "I guess not." Dikar was looking at the flattened-down grass where Yosuke had lain. He could see the vines that had been around his ankles, and even from here he could see that their ends were not frayed, but sliced through clean.

"No, Bessalton," Marilee murmured. "I guess There was nothing else you could do."

"That's what Franksmith told me," said Bessalton.

Marilee caught and clung to Dikar's hand; and he felt a shudder run through him.

"Franksmith," Bessalton said again. Her forehead wrinkled and her eyes were suddenly puzzled. "But—but Franksmith is dead. He is dead an' buried, up there on Clingman's Dome. How could he tell me anything?"

Marilee's breath hissed. She let go of Dikar, held her hand out to Bessalton. "Give me the knife, dear," she said very gently. "Please give it to me."

Looking at her, Bessalton was very white and Dikar could see that a sob was tearing at her throat; she shook like an aspen leaf in the fall's first chill breeze. Marilee took the knife from Bessalton's fingers and gave it to Dikar, and put her arm around the black-haired girl's waist. "Come dear," she said softly. "Come with me." She turned Bessalton away from the still form on the ground, led her off. Bushes parted, closed behind them.

Dikar stared where they had gone, his throat dry. This was a mess. They couldn't take Bessalton along with them, that was certain, but they couldn't send her back alone, either. Maybe Marilee could help him figure out what to do. Meantime, he'd better wipe the blood off this knife.

He bent and stuck it deep in the ground, and when he pulled it out it was clean again. Then, to keep himself from thinking about Bessalton, he cut branches from the bushes, piled them over the Asafric. Just as he finished, Marilee came back to him.

"She cried herself to sleep," she answered his silent question.

"We've got to get rid of her, Marilee, somehow. Some night she's liable to hear Franksmith tell her to kill you or me—"

"No, Dikar. She'll never again hear Franksmith talkin to her."

"How do you know?"

"I don't know how I know, but I'm sure of it as I am that you love me. Somethin' happened to Bessalton when she killed Yosuke, somethin' that shook her up so that— Listen!" Marilee's pupils got big, all of a sudden; black " and frightened. "What's that sound?"

Dikar heard it too—a blurring rumble, somewhere inland. "Sounds like a truck's runnin' along that road." They listened, and the rumble got closer, louder. "It'll go by, Marilee."

But it didn't. It was slowing. It stopped. A door slammed and bushes threshed as men pushed into them. "They've found us," Marilee whispered. "Dikar! They've found out we're here an' they've come for us."

CHAPTER 12
SURRENDER, AMERICAN

"THEY'VE GOT us cut off," Dikar declared, low-toned. "We can't get past 'em. We're trapped on this point."

"The river!" Marilee whispered. "The boat's—"

"Our only chance. Come on."

They flitted through the thicket. Marilee left Dikar for an instant and came back with Bessalton, whose face was muzzy with sleep. Dikar handed the black-haired Girl her knife, glanced at Marilee to make sure she had hers, and his own. These knives were all they had to fight with if they had to fight. There was nothing else.

The Black's rifles and Yosuke's revolver were at the bottom of the river. Dikar's own gun must be too, he hadn't been able to find it.

He let Marilee get a little ahead, so that she could lead the way to where she'd hidden the boat. The first loud threshing back of them had stopped. Dikar could hardly hear the Asafrics at all. That was bad. It meant that they must be Black trailers, whose woodcraft nearly matched that of the Bunch.

Marilee stopped suddenly, very carefully let a branch that she'd pulled aside drop back into place. She turned and her face was drawn, pallid.

"No use," she breathed. "There's a couple of little boats out there on the river, filled with soldiers."

"They've outguessed us!"

"No. They're only fishing, but they're right opposite the willow." Her brow wrinkled. "Listen. Those others aren't comin' down here after us. They seem to have stopped movin'."

Dikar cocked his head, listened. "Does sound like that. I'm goin to see what—" He darted away, slipping through the thorny tangle. With those clothes on he couldn't move as noiselessly as he'd liked, but the wind in the leaves made a louder rustle than he did.

The wind brought him the smell of Asafric Blacks. That scent swerved him toward where he'd seen the old house. He froze as a yell, high-pitched like the voices of all the Yellow officers, pierced the rustling hush.

"Come out of there." It was around on the other side of where Dikar knew the old house stood. "You are surrounded."

"Surround and be damned!" Wall-muffled, that was a ringing and defiant shout and the voice was that of an American. "If you want me, come and take me."

Instinct rather than anything he'd heard made Dikar turn his head. The Girls had followed him. "If we have to take you," the Asafric was answering the American, "you'll be sorry you ever was born. You'd better come out, unarmed."

Dikar jerked his hand to the Girls to go back. "Wait for me," the American shouted, "I'll be out with the first snowfall." Marilee crept closer to Dikar. "Can we help him, Dikar?"

"I'll see if there's a chance. You two stay here." He was moving again, around to the other side of the house from where the Asafric was yelling, "I shall give you five minutes to come out." Maybe he'd lied about the house being surrounded. "Five minutes, American, and then we come in after you."

A laugh, hoarse, mocking, was the only answer.

DIKAR WENT rigid, his nostrils flaring. Just ahead of him a dark bulk crouched in the greenery, a long, thin rifle barrel jutting sideways out from it. Somewhat beyond, there was another Black.

"Five minutes, American, counting from now."

Through shimmering green, Dikar could make out the house, its walls silvery-gray except where some flecks of paint still stuck to them, the windows glassless, black and empty-looking, the roof squashed as if a giant's foot had stepped on it.

Around the house was a space, twenty feet or so wide, where only grass and weeds grew, but no bushes. No one could cross that without making himself a plain target for the American inside. And the American seemed ready.

That was why the Asafric officer was trying to get him to come out. And that was why he had been silent since his last brave laugh. He couldn't watch all around the house at once, but if he kept quiet there was no telling where he was. He could surely kill two or three Blacks before they got him. Their officer was smart to try and save them if he could.

The one nearest Dikar had eyes for the house only. A fellow could sneak up… Dikar shook his head, telling himself he had no right to. He had no right to risk the fate of all Americans to save one.

The Black was moving. He took his hat off, put it on the end of his rifle, stuck it out of the bushes, just a little, so it looked like he was putting his head out, carelessly.

No shot came from the house. The American wasn't watching this side.

"Four minutes more," the yell came from the other side of the house. "You have four minutes to think it over."

Leaves rustled. The Asafric Dikar watched was lifting from his crouch. The other one did the same. Half-bent, rifles slanted across in front of their burly forms, they were prowling towards the house.

They weren't going to wait for the five minutes to be up.

DIKAR FELT a blinding surge of anger. Next thing he knew he was out in the open and his knife was flashing, had buried itself in the back of the nearest Black.

He pulled it out, twisted to the other, saw white, goggling eyes, thick, purplish lips opening. Before the slow-thinking Asafric could quite realize that this dark man in green was an enemy, Dikar had leaped at him, had sliced his throat.

The green-uniformed body thudded to the ground and Dikar was back in the bushes. "Three minutes," he heard the officer yell. "Only three minutes more." And then Dikar saw Marilee's white, big-eyed face. Bessalton's.

"We're in for it now," he snapped at them. "When the rest find those bodies… You two go around that way." He pointed. "Take care of any Blacks you find there. I'll take the other two sides."

They nodded, were off. Dikar was a silent shadow now in spite of his clothes, flitting through the tangle. He spotted a Black and dropped to his belly, slithered up on him like a snake, struck like a snake.

Dikar's next victim saw him. His scream was in his eyes as he died.

"One minute." The officer, flat under a bush, was the only one around in front of the house. "One minute, American, and we close in on you." He was little, wiry. Watch in one hand, revolver in the other, he was looking at the closed door of the house, at the broken steps leading down from it. "You cannot escape." There was no sound from inside the house. "Give up, Americ—"

The officer's back wasn't as tough to Dikar's knife as the muscled backs of the Blacks.

DIKAR FELT like he was going to be sick to the stomach, but the Girls' eyes were shining in their pale faces. "I know," Marilee said, seeing what he looked like. "I know what you're thinkin'. It didn't seem like fair fight, but it was.

"We weren't up against only the seven Asafrics here, our knives against their guns. If we'd given one of them a chance to even yell or shoot, the ones out there on the river would have heard the fightin' an' come to see what was up. We are up against the whole Asafric army, just the three of us, an' any way that we can find to even the odds is fair."

We Boys live by a code, Dikar thought, as he lifted to his feet, but Girls cut straight through codes when they have to. "We'll have to get away from here quick now, before others come to see what happened to this detachment."

"How about the American in there?"

"I'll go tell him he's safe." Dikar started toward the house.

A gun cracked inside of it and something plucked at Dikar's sleeve as he jumped back into the thicket. A great, ringing laugh followed him.

"Come on!" the laugh broke into shouted words. "Why don't you come on? I can't kill all of you. Come on an' take me."

"He saw your green uniform," Marilee exclaimed. "He thinks you're an Asafric. But we don't dare yell to him. Those soldiers on the river... Bessalton!" She grabbed at the other Girl, but was too late. Bessalton was out there in the open, walking straight toward the house, an odd little smile touching the corners of her mouth.

"Oh, gosh," Dikar groaned. "She's gone nuts again."

"No, she hasn't," Marilee was smiling too. "He can see that she's white. Oh, look at her, Dikar!"

The black hair rippled down around the slender, graceful figure, bare-legged, bare-armed, the white sarong outlining every lovely curve. Bessalton's head was high and proud as she walked in the sun.

"The door's opening," Marilee whispered. Bessalton reached the steps and the door up top of them came wide, and a lean, long-legged man was framed in the opening. He stared at Bessalton.

"I didn't feel the bullet." Dikar could hear him plainly.

"The bullet?" Bessalton sounded puzzled, looking up at the man. His hands were tight on the rifle he held across in front of a faded-blue shirt, open at the throat, and almost as ragged as the dirt-colored pants fastened around his waist by a belt of rope. His jaw was black with beard-stubble, his cheeks sunken, his eyes like burned-out coals.

"What bullet?" Bessalton asked.

"The one that killed me. I'm dead, ain't I?" He chuckled, and there was something suddenly gay in the sound of it, something heartwarming. "I must be. You couldn't be anyone but an angel, come to take me to Heaven."

Bessalton's laugh was startling. "Oh, Dikar," Marilee breathed. "She hasn't laughed since" Franksmith died."

CHAPTER 13
SOUTH TO PERIL

THE GAUNT young man closed the door after he'd let them into the house, but there was still enough light to see that there was dust everywhere in the desolate, empty rooms; to see that the slats, where the plaster had fallen out of the walls, like a grid of fishbones.

"Yeah," he chuckled. "It's an awful dump, but it sure looks good to Jim Corbin." He was grinning, but his eyes watched Dikar warily and he held his rifle ready to shoot. "All-fired good, considering that a couple minutes ago I thought I wouldn't be looking at anything by this time."

"You don't have to keep your finger curled on your gun trigger." Marilee smiled. "We're friends. Honest we are."

"You seem to have proved that, all right." He backed up against the wall beside the door and the way he stood, on one leg, the other a little lifted, he reminded Dikar of a fawn he'd cornered once on the Mountain, intending to catch and tame it for a pet for Marilee. "But I don't get it. I don't get it at all. Why should an Asafric—"

"I'm not an Asafric, Jim Corbin," Dikar grinned. "I'm as good an American as you are. My name's Dikar."

"Dikar! The hell you are!" Jim Corbin's gun-muzzle swung around to bear on Dikar's chest. "I've heard all about Dikar. He's got golden hair and yours is black, and— What kind of stunt are you trying to pull on me, anyway?"

"No stunt, cross my heart an' hope— Wait!" Dikar thought of something. "I know why you're hidin' here, inside the enemy lines. You're an agent of the Secret Net!"

"So what? That's no secret any more, judging from the visitors I was entertaining a little while ago. I belong to the Secret Net and my call's V-four, and where does that bring us?"

"To where I can prove I'm no Asafric." Dikar smiled. "Listen. Johndawson—he was V-six when I first found him in the Far Land—once told me that there's a question you of the Net ask to test if a station has been captured an' is bein' operated by a spy. That right?"

"Right enough. What about it?"

"If you ask it, I'll give you the answer."

"You will, hey?" Jimcorbin looked uncertain. "Well—how many feathers in the eagle's tail?"

"Thirteen, an' the risin sun may have scorched his wings, but he'll fly again into the red-striped mornin', up an' up till the white stars blaze in the blue sky. Is that right, Jimcorbin?"

"Right as rain," the other said, "and if you know that, you're no Asafric. Shake, Dikar." He shifted his rifle to his left hand and stuck out his right. Dikar's met it in a strong clasp.

"This is good." Jimcorbin's voice shook, and then he was laughing, all of a sudden.

"What's funny?" Dikar felt a little sore.

"Nothing. Only I just thought how close I was to kicking this slat down here." He jerked his head down at a hole in the plaster, right where his lifted foot had been. "That would have set off a charge of dynamite in the cellar, fixed there to blow up my radio set and this whole shebang, with everyone in it, when, as and if I was ever raided.

"Here I've sweated blood for three lonely, terrible years just trying to do a little bit for my country and I'd have wound up by blowing sky-high the guy that's done more for it than anyone except General Fenton himself. Not to speak of—" His look went to Bessalton and came away. "Hell, Dikar. Can't you see how funny that would have been?"

"No." Dikar shook his head. "I can't."

"BUT I can see something else," Marilee put in. "I can see that if we keep on foolin' around in this house, you'll get your chance to kick that slat. How much longer do you think it's goin' to be before someone's sent from Memphis to find out why those soldiers haven't come back?"

"Oh Lord," Jimcorbin groaned. "You're right. We'd better be kiting out of here, an' pronto. Look. If we move quick, we can make it up-river to V-two's shack, at Tennemo, without getting spotted, and that's inside our own lines. What are we waitin' for? Let's get started."

"You get started, Jimcorbin," Dikar said. "We're hidin' somewheres near here till it gets dark. We're not goin' up the river, you see. We're goin' down it. To the Gulf."

"To the Gulf!" Jim stared. "Why in the name of Luke and the other eleven Apostles would yo want to go there, and how the blazes do you think you're going to get there?"

"I can't tell you why, my friend, except that it's not because we've got a hankerin' to swim in salt water. An' I know as little as you do as to how. All I know is that at least one of us has got to get there, an' so one of us will. So I guess it's goodbye." Dikar stuck out his hand again.

Jimcorbin didn't take it. "Okay," he grunted. "If it's down-river, it's down-river. You're not shaking me." Once more his eyes went to Bessalton, and this time they stayed on her. "Not if I can help it."

"Nothin doin'." Dikar hated to say it. "You can't—"

"Wait," Marilee exclaimed. "Wait, Dikar. Jimcorbin! That truck out there, that the Asafrics came in—can you drive it?"

"And how!"

"Then we can get a uniform off one of the dead Asafrics, dress Jimcorbin up in it. His hair's black already. I saw only one tree out behind this house, but that's a walnut. I can make a dye from its bark that will stain his skin as dark as yours. You'll both look like Abyssinians. You can tie us Girls up in the back of the truck. We can be your prisoners, an' you're takin' us South."

"By Jerusalem!" Jimcorbin said softly, "It might work. I've heard the Asafrics are careless, down deep in their own territory, so if we can only get through this zone around here, where the truck might be recognized... I know all the backroads from here to salt water. I've had to know where our agents are posted. What do you say, Dikar? Shall we try it?"

"It's crazy." Dikar looked from Jimcorbin's face to Marilee's excited one. Inside his head he was hearing a tired, old voice that said, "I cannot believe that if we need a miracle to save America, He will not help us to work that miracle."

And Dikar was thinking how everything seemed to fit into Marilee's scheme: the Asafrics with their uniforms and their truck, Jimcorbin to drive it, even that the one tree near the house should be a walnut tree. It was as if He had brought Dikar and the Girls here, had sent the Asafrics here to take Jimcorbin, all at exactly the same time because that was His way of working the miracle Normanfenton prayed for.

"It's the craziest idea anyone ever heard of," Dikar said slowly. "We'll try it. Get busy, everybody."

Even in here he could hear the sound of the river, the endless rush of its waters, but somehow it was a friendly sound now, a sound that told him he was doing right.

There were four now, not one, and the river had brought them together. They were four, and they were going south with the flow of the river, to work a miracle that America might have a tomorrow.

FROM: *A History of the Asiatic-African World Hegemony, Zafir Uscudan, Ph.D. (Bombay) LL.D, (Singapore) F.I.H.S., etc. Third Edition, vol. 3. Chap XXVII pp991ff*

...The thousand and one versions of the legend of Dikar have brought down to us as many differing accounts of his amazing Odyssey from Memphis to the Mississippi's mouth, but diligent research fails to unearth a single detail sufficiently authenticated to merit repetition in a scholarly history of the time.

It would be surprising if the contrary were true. Men were not concerned with writing history in those days when the

Great Insurrection approached its apogee. They were making it.

The guerilla bands with which the Americans had begun their fight for freedom were at last coalescing into recognizable armies that had driven the Asafrics out of a wide swath of territory stretching across mid-Continent from the Atlantic Seaboard to the Rockies' eastern slope.

In far-off Panama, Viceroy Yee Hashamoto's tanks were setting out on their drive up through Central America and Mexico and Texas to destroy the presumptuous slaves. Benighted Europe…

…In all the documents that we have examined, we can find only two references to Dikar's mission. The first is this poignant entry in General Norman Fenton's diary:

> May 20: Today entrusted to Dikar my only hope of saving the Cause from complete disaster. Can any prospect so nebulous be called a hope? Even if he wins unscathed through six hundred miles teeming with Hashamoto's black and yellow troops, even if he somehow devises a way to cross the Gulf, what awaits him?
>
> Have I just sent that fine lad to his death with no reason to justify me except sheer desperation? A dozen years ago an uncertain number of our people, fleeing the invaders, were swallowed up by the dark jungle of the Quintana Roo. Since that day no word from them has ever reached the outer world.
>
> Do they still live? What have they become? What right have I to think that even if they still exist and can be roused to aid us, they can accomplish anything against the armored juggernauts of the Asafrics?
>
> Only He can answer Who has brought us thus far on the road to a free Tomorrow. Devoutly, humbly, I place in His hands the fate of this nation that has suffered so much.
>
> If He fail us—but that must not be. It cannot be.

The other bit of authentic data is a page from the log of Station V-2 of the Secret Net, at Tennemo, Tenn. A code message received here at 11:38 A.M., May Thirtieth, from

Operative V-4, James Corbin, reveals that Dikar inexplicably had been joined by his wife, Mary Lee (Marilee) and another girl of Dikar's Bunch, Elisabeth Alton (Bessalton).

These had just rescued Corbin from an Asafric raid on his station near Memphis. The two men disguised as Abyssinians, the girls posing as their prisoners, they were about to attempt to penetrate the enemy's territory in an army truck captured from the raiding party.

> We're going to blow up the station, (the message continues) and with it the bodies of the Asafrics who tried to take me, together with that of an extra Dikar killed earlier today.
> That last we're going to dress up in my clothes and make sure that he's messed up enough that he'll be counted for me. We're hoping that anyone sent to find out what's keeping the detachment won't notice that the ruins of the truck are no-where in the mess.
> "That way, with luck, there will be no hue and cry after us and we might have a chance to get away with this nutty stunt. Well, OM, thirty. When you hear the boom, look over this way and maybe you'll see old V-4 go up in a cloud of smoke.

That smoke-cloud veils the intrepid quartet from our sight. When it thins again to again permit us a glimpse of them, it is four days later and they are somewhere in that dim region of swamp and bayou on the border of Barataria Bay where centuries before Jean Lafitte and his buccaneers held forth....

CHAPTER 14
MIRROR OF THE WORLD

THE TREE Dikar climbed was like something in a dream. It was very like any one of the hemlocks on the Mountain, where he'd grown up and, in a strange way, it was very different.

It had a straight, tall trunk. Its branches forked and forked again till they became twigs, and the twigs were fringed with short, stubby green needles like a hemlock's.

But this tree had round, purple-colored fruit where a hemlock would have cones. It stood straddled high above a brooding lake on roots like gray, knobbed knees. Its bark was loose on its trunk in long, gray shreds and, strangest of all, its branches were festooned with some gray, dry-seeming stuff like looped beards that made the tree seem old, older than Time itself and vaguely frightening.

As Dikar climbed the tree, his legs and arms were heavy, the way one's legs and arms seem in a dream, and he was wet with sweat. That was because the air was so heavy in this land, steamy and hard to breathe.

This land to which, following the course of the river, they had come was all strange as this tree. It was choked with plants of a kind Dikar had never before seen, dark green and strange-leaved and murmursome.

Dark little streams wandered slow through it, sullen and silent, very different from the cheerfully babbling little streams on the Mountain. A strange smell hung about the streams and the glowering lakes, into which they spread.

Dikar reached the top of the tree. He saw the sky.

Even the sky was strange in this strange land. It was big and empty and it pressed down close on the lush green land and the land seemed to crouch under it, afraid. It was a strange, strange color, a sort of reddish yellow like metal heated, and no wind came out of it.

He hadn't come up here to look at the sky, Dikar reminded himself. He'd come up to look along the road down which their truck had rocked and slithered last night till the Girls had cried out that they couldn't stand it any more and Jimcorbin had stopped it beside the black glimmer of a half-seen lake.

DIKAR COULD make out the road for a little way, where it followed the edge of the lake, but then it curved back into the queer green woods and he couldn't see it any more.

It was little more than a path, black mud with green things sprouting out of it. Nothing moved on the part of the road he could see, and from where the road vanished he could hear no sound of life.

No sound of human life came to Dikar, and that was what he'd hoped for. But no sight, no sound of living beasts or birds came to him, though the night just ended had been noisy with startling screams, spine-chilling roars, little scutterings.

It was as if between the end of night and dawn all the wild things had fled something awful that was going to happen. That sky… Dikar shrugged, wiped sweat from his forehead with the back of his hand, started to climb down. He was a sissy, letting himself be scared by the way a sky looked. Why, there wasn't so much as a cloud in it.

He slid down to one of the tree's gray knees, sprang across four feet of water to the bank where Marilee and Bessalton stood, each holding two of the rifles they'd taken from the Asafrics. Just beyond them was the truck, and from its driver's seat Jimcorbin looked a question at Dikar.

"All clear," Dikar answered it. "Go ahead."

The noise of the starting motor was awful loud in the green hush. Jimcorbin twisted the steering wheel and the truck was moving, turning on the road. The wheels crunched the greenery of the lake's bank and went into the water and the truck went out into the water.

Greenish light trailed the truck wheels like the dark water had turned to a queer, liquid fire where they moved. Jimcorbin patted the steering wheel with his hand, said, " 'Bye, baby," and jumped from his seat, landed alongside the others.

The truck kept going, that strange green glow rippling where its wheels passed. All of a sudden its nose dipped and it slid slowly, almost as if it knew what was happening, under the water.

Where it had been, was only a great pool of green glow on the surface of the dark water. That faded, was gone.

"YOU FIGURED right," Dikar said. "It got to the edge of that deep hole we found with sticks this morning, before the water drowned its motor."

"Yeah. She did all right." Jimcorbin, tall in his green Asafric uniform, his face dark with the walnut stain Marilee had put on it, looked unhappy. "You know something, Dikar? I feel like I've murdered an old friend."

He chuckled suddenly, the little laughing lights in his brown eyes once more that had never quite gone out of them. "Will you listen to Jim Corbin getting sentimental over a bunch of steel and wood! Well, Dikar, the Gulf's about a mile from here, that way, and the truck's gone, so you're in charge from now on. What's next on the program?"

"Get to the Gulf, of course, an' find some way to get across it. Come on."

He took his rifle from Marilee and Jimcorbin took his from Bessalton, and they got started. The path went on and on through the green hush of these dim woods, and turned and got so narrow that they had to go single file, Dikar leading, Jimcorbin bringing up the rear.

They crossed a stream on the bridge of a fallen log, and when they'd gone a little way further the path bent sharply around a big tree like the one Dikar had climbed, and he saw light ahead, striking through the tangle.

The light grew stronger. Dikar pushed through a bush that stretched its twigs across the path.

All of a sudden there were no more leaves, no more trees. There was only the strange, reddish-yellow sky ahead of him, overhead and out in front, and rounding down under—

No. Above and in front of Dikar was the sky, but what was under the sky was water, stretching out and out till it met the sky, the water so still, so smooth, that it was like the mirror into which he'd looked while he'd blackened his golden hair and beard, and just the way that mirror had pictured his face, the water pictured the sky.

The Girls came out of the woods and Dikar heard their breath catch in their throats as they stopped stockstill beside him.

SAND SLOPED down from their feet to the water, and then the water began and went out, on and on endlessly, and there was no other shore out there but only the reddish-yellow water and the reddish-yellow sky rounding down to meet it, sky and water enclosing a space unthinkably vast and empty.

The water heaved slowly, Dikar saw now, as if the world itself breathed in deep sleep, and halfway up the round of the sky an immense scarlet ball was the nightmare sun of the sleeping world's dread-filled dream.

This sand at whose edge they stood ran away from them, left and right, curving outward till it became two long points of land that reached out into the water, black against the reddish-yellow glow, like two great arms embracing the water. But the water stretched away between the ends of the arms into that vast and lonely nothingness.

"The end of the world," Marilee murmured, her voice low, hushed. "We've come to the end of the world, Dikar."

Jimcorbin chuckled. "Not quite, kid. Not quite the end of the world. Just the Gulf of Mexico."

"The Gulf!" Dikar exclaimed. "But where's Yucatan?"

"Due south, m'lad. Straight ahead the way we're facing."

"Straight ahead? Why can't we see it then?"

"Because after about thirty miles, your line of sight skids off the round of the earth—"

"The earth isn't round, it's flat. Look." Dikar waved his arm out in front of him. "You can see that it's as flat as—well, it's flat."

"Holy mackerel! Don't tell me you never learned—no," Jimcorbin checked himself. "There wasn't anyone on that Mountain of yours to teach you." They'd told him all about their Mountain, on the way down.

In the torch-glow they saw a man lying in agony at the idol's feet.

"Well, you'll just have to take my word for it. The earth's round, and that's why the horizon, that line where the sky seems to meet the water, is only about thirty miles from here, but the Gulf goes on and on about five hundred miles more, and then there's Yucatan, where you want to go."

"Five hundred miles," Dikar repeated, dismayed. "That's almost as far as we've come already. I knew, it was too far to swim, but five—" He broke off. "What's that, noise?"

JIMCORBIN COCKED his head and listened to the quick *pop-pop-pop* that had suddenly rapped against the brooding hush. "I'd say it was an auxiliary motor someone's been having trouble with an' has just managed to get started again. The boat it's on is hidden from us by that headland."

He pointed to the arm of land on the left. "By the same token we're hidden from whoever's on it. Now if by some miracle we could get hold of that, Dikar, it would be a better way of getting across the Gulf than swimming."

"By some miracle. It's funny you should say that, Jimcorbin. That's exactly what Normanfenton said he was going to pray for, some miracle to help me."

"Prayer's no good any more, Dikar, in this lousy world—Get back! Hide, everybody! That damned lugger's coming around the headland!"

They jumped back into the bushes, just far enough to screen them, and then they were peering through the green curtain at the boat that poked its nose into view far out there, and was skimming the glassy surface of the Gulf.

"Oh she's a beauty," Jimcorbin breathed. "A thirty-five footer if she's an inch, sloop-rigged, and as clean lines as I've ever seen. That one was never built in an Asafric yard, not on your life."

"There are Asafrics on her now, though." Dikar liked the boat too. Low to the water, it was like a white bird. "I can see three of them. Yellow. They are officers."

"You've got good eyes, guy, if you can make out the color of their skin, though even I can see the green of their uniforms. They must have been caught in the calm," Jimcorbin mused, "and then found that their pusher was *kaput*. The devil! They're putting about. Now what?"

"They're coming in here!" Marilee's fingers were cold on Dikar's wrist. "They're goin to land right here. We've got to get away quick!"

Jimcorbin laughed a little, harshly. "Looks like you're right. They're sure heading straight for this cove. But that's nothing to get all hot an' bothered about. It will take them twenty minutes or more, the rate they're traveling. However, I guess we'd better be going on our way. How about it, Dikar?"

"Ugh?"

"I asked how about our getting started away from here?"

Dikar looked around at him eyes narrowed, brow knitted. "We're not goin' away, Jimcorbin. We're goin to stay here an' wait for 'em."

"Wait for— Are you clean out of your noodle?"

"No. You just said that prayer's no good any more, in this lousy world. Well, you're wrong. Normanfenton prayed for me to find a way to get to Yucatan, an' there's the answer to his prayer. That boat's goin' to take us there."

"Could be." Jimcorbin whispered. "Could very well be. There are four of us an' only three of them, an' even if they are armed, we can pick them off with our rifles as they come in.

"It's taking an awful chance. The sound of firing will carry for miles across the water. It's sure to be heard at Port Eads or Morgan City, or both, and unless the Asafrics are dumber than I think, there'll be a destroyer out to see what the shooting's for. Those babies are fast. They'll overhaul that sloop in nothing flat, and—"

"There ain't goin to be any shootin'," Dikar said quietly. "Listen. Listen to me, all of you."

CHAPTER 15
WARNING IN THE SKY

THE *PUT-PUT-PUT* got louder as the boat came in between the arms of land. Then it stopped, but peering through the leaves, Dikar saw that the boat still came on toward the shore, the water parting for it, sliding along the clean, long curve of its sides.

A very fat Yellow officer stood by the pole that stuck up out of its middle, a thin one stood up in the very front, leaning over and looking down into the water, and there was another one in the back.

The one in the front yelled something all of a sudden, and the one in the back dropped something into the water. The boat stopped moving, its nose very near the shore. The thin Asafric climbed out on the nose of the boat and jumped. He landed on the sand and then the other two jumped.

They came up on the sand a little way and looked around, as

if they didn't know where they were. The fat Asafric's face was round and greasy, and his slant eyes were very little.

The one who had been at the back of the boat limped a little. He turned to look out over the water and jabbered something in his high-pitched voice. The others turned and jabbered, as if they were excited and happy and frightened all at the same time.

Dikar tried to see what they were looking at, but all he could see was a tiny black cloud, way off on the horizon. He shrugged, stepped sideways into the road and walked out on the sand.

He'd left his rifle in the bushes, but he'd made sure his Asafric uniform was fixed straight, all the buttons buttoned. Though his hair and beard had grown a little so that some gold showed at the roots, he was sure no one would notice it unless they came very close.

He kicked a shell on the sand with his bare foot, stopped and stood very straight as the thinnest of the Asafrics wheeled around, his hand darting to the revolver butt in his belt.

Dikar snapped his right hand up to his head and down again, the way he'd seen the Black-soldiers do that time in Newyork. The fat officer's fingers dropped away from his gun. His high-pitched voice jabbered something that Dikar couldn't understand.

Dikar grinned, made noises with his mouth that sounded like they meant something but didn't really. Doubletalk. The Yellows stared at him, puzzled-looking. Dikar smiled, kind of sheepish, said. "Yoh no un'stan Abyssin talk, sah?"

"Is that what you are?" the thin one asked. "An Abyssinian?"

"Yaas, sah. Me Abyssin boy f'om Mountains ob Moon. Me belong Cap'n Tsi Huan." This was the name of a real Asafric officer who Dikar knew led a company of Abyssinians. "Cap'n sen me—"

"Never mind all that. Can you guide us to the closest point where there are substantial buildings?"

"Oh yaas, sah!"

"Very well. You will do so, at once. We do not wish to be caught— Get moving, boy!"

"Yaas, sah." Dikar snapped his hand up to his head again. "Dis way. He turned and started off along the path.

THE SQUELCH of shoes in the muck told him the Yellows were following, and he did not have to look back to know that the tangled, thick greenery forced them to walk single file.

Dikar speeded up his long strides, got way ahead of the first officer. He went around the big trees at the sharp bend in the path—dropped to hands and knees and crawled under a bush beside, the path.

"Not so fast!" the thin officer's thinner voice called. "We don't want to lose you."

He came around the tree. A green length of vine stretched across the road caught under his chin. A bent-down tree bough, above, snapped up, lifted the Asafric straight up in the air as his frantic hands clawed at the noose that had tightened around his neck.

He had time for a single, agonized scream before the trap, like those Dikar had so often set for rabbits but much bigger, cut off his breath. The fat man plunged into sight, reaching for his gun. Dikar's hands shot out from his covert, clamped on muddy ankles, jerked. The Yellow squealed, squashed down into the mud. Dikar leaped on his back and seized the soft throat.

A crunching thud told him that Jimcorbin, hiding the other side of the path, had brought his rifle-butt down on the head of the third Asafric. The Yellow officer pinned under Dikar struggled frantically, but Dikar's fingers tightened. The roll of yellow fat at the back of the thick neck turned slowly purple. A long quiver ran through the soft body, and then it was very still. High over it a thinner corpse swayed, back and forth with the tree's gray, looped beards.

Dikar unbent his stiffened fingers, shoved up to his feet, turned and went back past the tree. He jumped over what lay in the path there. Jimcorbin's face was gray, his mouth straight and thin-lipped. "Remind me about my father," he begged Dikar. "Remind me how my father died."

"I'm remindin' myself about all the American men an' women who have died since the Asafrics came an' how they died, an' how the rest have lived. An' I'm remindin' myself about the Asafric tanks, that will soon be startin' out from Panama."

Dikar shook himself and then he was whistling *bob-o-link, bob-o-link,* the way he used to on the Mountain when, after supper and dishwashin', he wanted to call Marilee away from the Bunch.

Bob-o-link the answer came. In the dim, green hush it seemed a strange sound. Dikar and Jimcorbin reached the path's end and the Girls met them there, their faces anxious.

"The boat is ours," Dikar told them, but only Marilee heard him, because Bessalton had ears and eyes only for Jimcorbin.

Dikar was able to smile again, seeing that, and Marilee smiled at him, and Dikar knew that they were both smiling because their friends had each found someone to end heartache and loneliness.

"COME ON, everyone," Dikar said. "Let's take the boat, now it's ours, an' start off. I suppose you can make it go like you could the truck, Jimcorbin."

"Surest thing you know." Jimcorbin grinned. "I can run that pusher an' I can sail her if we get a wind. I did plenty of both on old Misissip' when I was a youngster. But—I dunno." He looked out over the water. "I don't like the looks of this sky."

Dikar looked out there too, and the feeling that something terrible was going to happen was back. The awful emptiness, the color of the sky and water. That cloud on the horizon was a little bigger now, but only a very little, and there was still no wind.

"I don't like it either," he said, watching how the breathing of the water had gotten deeper, longer, "but we can't hang around here. Those Asafric officers must have come from somewhere nearby an' when they don't show up, their friends will be out lookin' for 'em. We've started somethin' we can't stop."

Jimcorbin nodded. "Let's go then."

The boat was bigger, when they got on it, than it had seemed from shore and it was all clean and shining everywhere. The girls ran around it, excited, but Dikar was too busy helping Jimcorbin and learning a lot of things about a boat, including a lot of new words.

He helped Jimcorbin pull up the thing the limping Asafric had thrown into the water. It was like a curved arrow of iron, pointed at both ends, with another long rod of iron fastened to the middle. This, Jimcorbin said, was an anchor.

He made Dikar coil up the rope very neatly on the boat's floor, that Jimcorbin called its deck. The tall pole, like a tree without branches, which stuck up from the middle of the deck was a mast; the sail was a huge cloth folded up and tied—reefed—to another pole that stuck out from the mast and was called a boom. The ropes that would open the sail—unfurl it—were sheets.

Toward the back—the stern—of the boat was a little engine. Dikar turned a big iron wheel on this while Jimcorbin fiddled with it. It wouldn't get started, and Dikar got mad and turned the flywheel around very fast and then it was going around by itself and the engine was *put-put-putting*.

Jimcorbin grinned, went to a sort of big wooden wheel with a lot of handles sticking out from it. He did something there. "Hey!" Dikar exclaimed, "The land's moving!" and then felt his face get red as Jimcorbin threw his head back and roared with laughter. It was the boat that was moving, of course, not the land.

The Girls stood by the rail, up in the prow of the boat, looking out across the Gulf. Dikar could make out only their outlines, slim and lovely against the weird glow of the sky, ankle-length hair rippling very gently in the stir of air through which the boat moved.

SO CLEAR was the water that the boat seemed not to be on its surface but to be floating in midair, that reddish-yellow, uneasy light under it as well as above. "You gals better duck in the cabin," Jimcorbin called, "till we get out of sight of land. Dikar an' I are all right in our uniforms, but if someone on shore with a glass spots you two—"

"Where's the cabin?" Marilee asked, looking around. "I don't see any."

"That little house, forward of the mast there."

"Oh!"

They went into it. Dikar stood straddle-legged to the slow rise and fall of the boat. "I've got a funny feeling," he said after a long while, "here in my stomach."

"It's going to get funnier," Jimcorbin said, grinning, "before you're much older. Say! I think there's wind coming! Off there!"

Dikar turned the way Jimcorbin pointed. They were out past the headlands. Far off to the east the water was no longer like a mirror. "Let's get the sail up," Jimcorbin said. "Here. I've got the wheel lashed. Give me a hand with these sheets. Hey!" His fingers tightened on Dikar's shoulder. "What's the matter? You gone deaf?"

"No," Dikar muttered, "No. I was just looking at that cloud. It's spreadin awful fast."

It had spread all along the eastern horizon. It was a black mass all rolling in on itself the way the smoke of wet wood does, and the edges of the billows were a bright yellow. "We're in for a storm," Jimcorbin muttered. "We'll get as much south-ing as we can before we have to reef sail again."

They got the sail up and the wind came and filled it. Jimcorbin stopped the engine. The boat flew through the water like a beautiful, great bird, the water hissing along its side.

Spray stung Dikar's cheeks, cold and bracing. He pulled great breaths of the stinging, fresh wind into his lungs which had been muffled so long by the hot, steamy air of the queer woods, and for a while he forgot the funny feeling in his stomach.

But the water got rougher and the boat rose and fell and the feeling came back. "I'm sick," he groaned. "Jimcorbin. I'm awful sick," and just then the Girls burst out of the cabin, their faces green, their eyes staring out of their heads. They ran to the rail, and the next moment Dikar was with them there.

Dikar hated Jimcorbin for his ringing laughter, and could cheerfully have killed him, but he was much too busy.

After a while Dikar felt a little better. "Go on into the cabin and lie down," Jimcorbin said. "I've already sent the Girls in."

Dikar was so weak he had to hold on to things and drag along the deck. Marilee lay groaning on a sort of shelf that ran along one wall of the cabin, inside, and Bessalton suffered on the one that ran along the other wall, so Dikar lay down on the floor and closed his eyes.

With his eyes closed he felt a little better and the slow rise and fall, rise and fall of the boat was soothing, and he fell asleep.

THE FOREST in which he wandered was dim and ominous, and the ground under his feet rose and fell, rose and fell, in a very strange way.

Marilee screamed somewhere and just then a black beast dropped down on Dikar and another leaped at him, clawing, and it was Marilee who'd fallen on him from her shelf and Bessalton was clawing at him, thrown clear across the cabin from hers, and the floor of the cabin slanted up from where they were all tangled. It was night and outside the cabin was a terrible, whistling howl and a loud cracking, and Jimcorbin shouting something Dikar couldn't understand.

Dikar got free of the Girls somehow, and somehow was climbing to the cabin door. It was shut. Something held it shut, something against which it took all his strength to force the door open.

It was the wind that had held the door shut, the wind that howled and pinned Dikar against the cabin wall, staring into a wild waste of water that slanted up into a night sky. Not night. A terrible sort of light filled the air, a lurid light, and the sky was a black mass rolling in on itself in tremendous billows edged with the yellow and terrible light.

That loud cracking was the sail and Jimcorbin was fighting with the sheets, his mouth open, shouting something to Dikar. The sail split into a hundred flapping ribbons that tore away from the mast.

Dikar fought up the slant of the deck, fought the wind, till he got one arm around the mast, to which Jimcorbin clung. "What?" he yelled. "What? Storm?"

"Storm, hell," Jimcorbin shouted in his ear. "This—is—a hurricane."

CHAPTER 16
HANDS OF THE HURRICANE

THERE WAS no up or down, no east or west. For an endless time the world had been nothing but a howling madness that beat Dikar into a sort of nightmare numbness.

Vaguely he knew that he still lived. Vaguely he knew that the shadowy shapes he saw now and then within some less violent flurry of the storm were Jimcorbin and Marilee and Bessalton. They'd gotten the girls out of the cabin in those first few frantic moments and lashed them with ropes to the mast.

There was no cabin any more. There was no mast, only a jagged stump sticking up out of the welter of foam that forever had been pouring across the deck, washing to Dikar's knees, to his waist, fighting to break the lashings that cut into him.

That tree-thick pole had snapped right through, feet over his head, and so great was the roar of the storm that he had not heard it. So great was the strength of the hurricane that the huge mast and its trailing ropes had soared almost straight up into the driving murk, like a dry leaf on fall wind, and so had not crushed the pigmy humans lashed to its splintered stump.

That had been very long ago. Since then a night must have come, a morning returned, because there had been a blackness and now there was this lurid, terrible glow. Or had there been many nights and mornings, or none? Dikar could not figure how long it had been. He could not think, could not feel. He was hardly Dikar at all, only a something half-drowned, half-stunned, too beaten to be even afraid.

And suddenly he *was* afraid. Suddenly, the boat was shivering beneath him, its fabric groaning, ready to break apart at last, each separate small inch of it screaming.

A loose rope-end slatted sharply, somewhere. Queer that Dikar could hear these small sounds above the deafening wind—and then he realized the amazing truth. There was no wind!

There was no wind, all of a sudden, and though about the crippled hulk a vast and foam-streaked waste heaved mountainously, water and air were separate again.

SLUMPED AGAINST his lashings, a head lolling, Dikar saw the water run from the deck and the deck appear, splintered but whole. He lifted his head, turned it to Marilee.

Water streamed from her wet and battered body, hair was soaked and stringy about her slimness, but her eyes lifted to meet his and in them he saw the same wild, unbelieving joy that he knew must be in his own eyes.

"It's over," he cried. "It's finished an' we're saved."

"Says you," Jimcorbin's voice was husky, tired to the point of agony but still held a shadow of his familiar chuckle. "I hate to disappoint you, lad an' lassies, but this isn't the end of the hurricane. We've simply come into its windless center, into the eye of the storm. In a little while it will come again from the other direction."

"Oh no," Marilee sobbed, "No, Jimcorbin. The boat can't live through much more."

"No, it can't. It can't live through another fifteen minutes of that kind of beating. Well, folks," his blue lips grinned, "it's been nice knowing you. I—"

"Jimcorbin!" Bessalton cried from the other side of the mast, "Dikar! Look. Off there!"

Dikar strained around against the tightness of the ropes, craned to see what it was toward which she flung out a tense, trembling arm. Heaving water. A wrack of cloud. A darker loom within the cloud, formless—

"Land," Jimcorbin gasped. "That's land!"

Marilee's hand somehow reached, clasped Dikar's. "Land," she whispered. "Do you hear, Dikar? It's land an' we're saved."

"Hold it," Jimcorbin said. "Hold everything. That shore, whatever it is, is two miles off, at least, maybe more. We're drifting parallel to it, or a little away, if anything. Our sail's gone an' even if we could rig one in the time we've got, there is no wind at all. How're we going to get to it?"

"The engine of course," Dikar was surprised he'd forgotten. "We'll get the engine started—"

"Take a look." Jimcorbin jerked his chin to the stern. Dikar looked there and saw a couple of twisted bolts sticking up from split boards, a broken pipe. Nothing else. "The pusher went overboard long ago, an' I'm afraid there are no oars aboard. Now, if we had wings, maybe—"

"We have arms, legs." Dikar fumbled at his belt. His knife was still in its pocket. "How long have we, Jimcorbin, before the storm swoops back?"

"An hour maybe. Maybe a little more."

"Time enough to swim there." The knife was already cutting Dikar free. "But we'll have to hurry."

JIMCORBIN WAS slashing the ropes that held him to the mast's stump while Dikar worked on Marilee's. Then, having freed Bessalton, Jimcorbin said: "No sharks, the storm will have sent them to the bottom. There's a chance, a bare chance of getting away with it."

Dikar tore off the rags the storm had made of his Asafric uniform. "Get undressed, Jimcorbin. Hurry up!" The Girls didn't need to be told. They'd slipped off their wet sarongs, were knotting their long hair in great bundles, brown, black, atop their heads. "What are you waitin for?"

Jimcorbin stared at the other side of the boat. "I—I—" he stammered, his face getting red. "I know I ought to, but—"

"But what?" Dikar snapped, wondering what had come over him. "We'll be racin' the storm an' every little thing that might slow us up must be got rid of."

"I know, but—"

Marilee caught Jimcorbin's arm, twisted him around to her. "You idiot," she blazed, madder than Dikar had ever seen her. "You're ashamed of seein' me an' Bessalton without clothes an' havin' us see you without 'em."

But still Dikar couldn't understand why Jimcorbin was troubled, just as he'd never understood why Walt had made the Bunch cover themselves up at Wespoint, the Boys with fawnskins an' the Girls with their sarongs. What was there about one's body to be ashamed of?

"What you ought to be ashamed of," Marilee was saying, "is the dirtiness that makes you ashamed."

"But—but Marilee—"

"Oh I know," she broke in. "It isn't your fault. You've been taught to think that the body God gave you is dirty, an' to be hidden, no matter what. Well," she shrugged, letting go of him. "If you'd rather be drowned then have Bessalton an' me see you naked, all right. But don't expect us to be such fools."

"You win." Jimcorbin grinned like a kid that's been caught doing some silly thing. He started to pull off his uniform.

DIKAR LIFTED an arm over his head and put it into the water and kicked. Eyes squinted shut against the salt burn of the water, he lifted the other arm and put it into the water and kicked.

He'd been doing this forever. Arm, kick. Arm, kick. He would keep on doing it forever. Arm, kick. He was tired, awful tired. Somewhere far off, there was a rumbling. The storm returning.

What was the use? Why not stop and sink peacefully into the green, quiet water, before the storm came.

"Look!" Jimcorbin's voice was in his ear. "Look there, Dikar."

Dikar opened his eyes. That mass, not far—strange trees, leaning, all branches stripped from them. Green stuff, fluttering. But the vast howling of the storm wind, nearing swiftly. "Come on! Come on, Marilee! Come on, everybody!"

Fast, fast, never mind how tired. Fast toward that smother of foam, that hollow boom of water on land. The water had a thousand hands plucking at Dikar to pull him back. The water had a thousand fists battering him. But he fought it.

He fought it and had an arm to help Marilee fight it and all of a sudden there was ground under his feet and he was dragging Marilee up out of the angry water and they were on land, no more water, and he knew that Jimcorbin and Bessalton were staggering beside them, and the rumble of the hurricane was coming closer.

"Keep going," Jimcorbin gasped. "We've got to find some sort of shelter. Keep going."

They were in the woods, staggering, stumbling away from the shore. They were threshing into the woods. There were smells in Dikar's nostrils, smells of soaked earth, of broken wood, sap oozing.

They were fighting through a nightmare tangle of greenery, twisted vines, uprooted trees. Queer trees, their trunks furred with red hair instead of bark. Queer leaves, long and narrow and spreading from a middle point like fingers of a spread hand. Or was it the swiftly deepening darkness that made them seem so queer? The lurid glow like the strange light of a dreadful dream?

"I—I can't go any further," Dikar heard Bessalton whimper, close behind, and heard Jimcorbin grunting, "You've got to. We've got to beat that storm—"

IT STRUCK! It pounced on the woods like some gigantic, howling beast and the woods exploded into an awful roar about them, filled with a crash of falling trees, a hail of flying splinters.

Dikar tightened his arm around Marilee, saw that her mouth was open, shouting something, but he could not hear her. Terror leaped into her eyes and she dragged back on him, her hands grabbing at him, pulling him to a stop.

Right here, right in front of Dikar, thunder crashed. No, not thunder! Where there had been only wind-threshed green a huge, furred tree-trunk lay; it would have struck him had Marilee not dragged him back.

It rocked, was trying to roll, would crush them if it rolled. They had to get away from it, but it blocked them off. Back then! They couldn't go back, another tree had crashed behind them, just behind Jimcorbin and Bessalton who stared at it, eyes dazed, mouths twisted grotesquely. The huge tree-trunks shielded them a little from the almost solid wind, but the rocking trunks were a greater danger. If one or both rolled just a little more....

Dikar looked to the right. The trees slanted to each other, blocked escape. To the left, then. The great masses of their roots had some space between. The roots were packed with earth. They must have left deep pits where they pulled out all that earth.

"This way!" Dikar shouted, but he knew that even Marilee, crushed to him, could not hear. He shoved her in the direction he wanted her to go, beat with his fists at Bessalton and Jimcorbin to make them understand. Frantically he drove them along between the rocking trees, past the root masses.

The full force of the solid wind hit them, but even in the half-night Dikar saw he'd been right. There were deep holes here where roots had spread for ages on ages. He threw himself against Marilee, Jimcorbin, and they all went down into one of the holes together, tumbled in slithery mud at its bottom.

The wind was not quite so bad; the shreds of the storm-ripped woods went by overhead. Dikar untangled himself from the floundering, mud-plastered bodies, lifted his head. He saw a black opening in the earth-wall to one side, blinked, hitched himself to it.

And then he was waving wildly to the others, his mouth forming a shout they could not hear. "A cave. It's a cave. We're saved."

They could not hear him but they saw what he wanted, floundered to him. Dikar shoved Bessalton past him into the black hole, then the two others, and he crawled into it himself.

It was black dark in there, and the roar of the storm was loud behind, but the storm no longer battered them.

DIKAR LAY panting. He lifted his head, all of a sudden, his nostrils flaring. The air in here smelled musty, dead, and by that Dikar knew that this was an old cave the roots and the trees had grown up to cover.

There was a smell of salt water too, strangely, and beneath the roar of the storm he could hear a hollow booming, like that which had pounded his ears before he'd gotten deep into the woods. That meant that somewhere this cave must have another opening to the Gulf.

These things flashed through Dikar's mind as he stared into the dark, but they were not what had brought his head up so sharply, not what made him stare so intently over the pale forms of his companions, into the dimness beyond. Another smell threaded the smells of rock and earth and ancient wood, a smell that frightened him.

What was it? It was not so dark any longer, in there. His eyes were getting used to the night and by the little light filtering in through the opening behind, he saw that the cave was narrow, too low for a man to stand upright, for a little way. But further in it widened. In that bigger part, he saw—

Blackness smashed down on him, with a tremendous crash. Bessalton screamed. "It's all right," Jimcorbin grunted. "All that's happened is that the palm's rolled over and its roots have closed up the entrance."

Dikar's skin was an icy sheath for his body. The way out was blocked! Naked, defenseless, they were shut in here with the dreadful thing he'd made out, deep there within the cave, in the instant before all light went.

CHAPTER 17
HOUSE OF THE GODS

THAT WHICH Dikar had seen, there in the blackness, had been man-shape in a bloated, hideous sort of way, but it had been high as two of the tallest men Dikar had ever seen, wide as four, and it had been gray all over, the gray of something long dead.

Its head was a full half of its height, neckless, squarish and thick through as its swollen-bellied body and it had the beak of a bird, the great hook-curved, sharp and cruel beak of an enormous eagle. Each side of that beak there was a black pit, round, huge, within which terrible eyes had seemed to lurk.

Something touched Dikar, and he whirled. But it was Marilee's hand. "What's the matter?" she demanded, her voice suddenly sharp against the muffled storm-roar. "What's scared you?"

"Nothin'," he grunted, pushing ahead of her a little, so that he'd be between her and that Thing. "I'm not scared. But be quiet. For the love of God, quiet."

Crouched, dry-mouthed, he strained to catch the smallest sound. The Thing's pointed ears, grotesquely small at the corners of its square head, had been perked in the instant he'd glimpsed it, as if it had been trying to separate the noises they made from the storm-howl, the far-off boom of storm-roused waters. Had it heard them? Was it creeping toward them now, silent, stealthy?

But it couldn't. It was too big, much too big, to get into this part of the cave where they were. It couldn't get at them. As long as they stayed here, they were safe.

Dikar let himself breathe again, even made himself laugh a little. "I thought—no tellin' what the storm might have driven in here," he said. "We'd better be careful, folks, keep close together, not move around at all till we can see where we're goin'. There might be snakes, or hidden holes in the cave-floor—"

"You *are* scared," Marilee broke in. "The way you're babblin', I know you're terrible scared, Dikar. You did see somethin'. What was it you saw?"

"Some shadow, I guess. Some trick of light an' shade."

"No, Dikar. Light an' shade don't smell like fresh-spilt blood."

That was it! That was what this smell was that had frightened him even before he saw the Thing.... What was that? What was that deep, hoarse noise?

"Someone groaned," Bessalton exclaimed. "I heard someone groan, way in there."

Jimcorbin made a queer sound with his throat. "Somebody's in there, badly hurt. Hear it?" From within the lightless secret depths the hoarse moan came again. "Must have been smashed during the first part of the storm, crawled in here. We've got to help him, Dikar. Come on."

THERE WAS a rattle of little stones as he lifted. "No!" Dikar flung out a terrified hand in that direction, caught hold of a stubbled jaw. "No, Jimcorbin. Don't move. Marilee! Bessalton! Don't any of you dare move from here."

"What the devil?"

"What is it, Dikar?" Marilee's calm, low voice asked. "Tell us what has you so scared. We have a right to know. We're not babies. What did you see, back there?"

"I don't know."

"That's crazy. You must know what you saw."

"I ought to, but I just don't believe it." Dikar told about it. "I think the worst part is its color," he ended. "Gray. Like dead wood, or weathered stone—"

A roar of laughter from Jimcorbin broke in on him, a howl of rollicking laughter. "I'm not kiddin!" Dikar flared, angry. "I did see that gray Thing back there!"

"Sure," Jimcorbin spluttered. "Sure you saw it, old man." He managed to stop laughing. "But it's nothing to be frightened of. It's gray like stone because it is stone. It's a statue carved out of stone and the men that carved it have been dead for at least six centuries, if I remember my archaeology right. What you saw was the statue of a Mayan god."

"Mayan? What—?"

"The Mayas were the people of a vanished civilization. By the Lord Harry! I just realized—that statue shows that we've reached exactly the place we were aiming for. Yucatan.

"This peninsula was the Mayas' last refuge and its jungle is full of their relics, huge pyramids like the one at Chichen Itza, temples, like the one at Uxmal, sacrificial wells. Your sculptured friend in there has probably had countless human sacrifices made to him in his time, but that sort of thing hasn't happened for hundreds of years—" He checked.

It was only a shadow of sound now, deep there in the blackness. A shadow of a word. "Help." Marilee's fingers dug into Dikar's arm. "Help!" The word whispered to them again.

"English," Marilee breathed. "Oh Dikar. It's an American that lies hurt in there an' he's heard us; he's callin' to us to help him. We've got to, Dikar. We've got to find an' help him."

"Yes. Sure. But we can't go plungin' in there, without bein' able to see a thing. We're liable to break a leg. Anythin' might happen. If only there was some way to get some light."

"There's pieces of dry wood, here where I am." That was Bessalton. "They feel like pieces of some root broken off when the tree fell."

"An there are all these loose stones around." Dikar felt better, now there was something to do. "Wait there, Bessalton. I'm comin' there to you."

HE FOUND her without trouble, cleared a space on the rock floor where she was, took some bits of root-bark from her and scratched fuzz from their inside surface with his fingernails. He made a little pile of this, felt for and picked up two stones, cracked them together near the fuzz.

Sparks flew, were gone. Dikar cracked the stones together again. They sparked, but nothing happened. He kept on doing this. He kept on doing it till his hands were sore, his fingers aching.

"No use," Jimcorbin sighed. "You're just wasting time, an' meanwhile that poor brute's stopped calling."

"Wastin' time, am I?" Dikar grunted. "Look." One of the countless sparks hadn't gone out. It glowed, a red dot in the black where the pile of fuzz was. Dikar's hands went down to it, he let his breath drift across it.

Nobody moved. Nobody spoke. The spot brightened, grew. Dikar dared to breathe a little more strongly. The pile of fuzz was all alight, and it throbbed like a bright red heart. Dikar broke a little splinter from the piece of bark in his hands, put it on the red pile. But it went dark.

"Now you've spoiled it," Jimcorbin groaned. But Dikar kept blowing, very carefully. At last a flame popped out of the splinter, yellow, no bigger than a fly's wing. Dikar held his breath and with his fingertips put another tiny splinter across the first. It caught. A third splinter spread the flame a little more. A fourth, quite a bit bigger.

Dikar's fire was growing swiftly. Now he could feed it the sticks Bessalton handed him, small ones at first, then bigger and bigger ones.

A small but healthy bonfire crackled on the cave's stony floor. Dikar sat back on his haunches, and grinned at Jimcorbin. The latter grinned back, "I apologize," he said. "Here." He thrust a piece of twisted root at Dikar, wrist-thick, about the length of his forearm. "This will make a good torch. Let's get it lit and go take a look-see."

The firelight threw black, wavering shadows on the rocky walls. Naked except for the mud with which they were plastered, crouched in the red glow, the four of them looked exactly like the people in a picture Walt once showed to Dikar of humans who lived on earth thousands and thousands of years ago.

Dikar lifted the root, its tip flaming now, said, "Come on, Jimcorbin. You Girls stay here by the fire an' wait for us."

"Like fun we will," Bessalton came back at him. "You two can go ahead, but we're goin' to be right behind you."

"But—"

"Stop arguin'," Marilee snapped. "I haven't heard the hurt man a long while now. If we waste any more time, we'll be too late to help him."

Dikar shrugged, picked up a fist-size stone from the rubble, waited for Jimcorbin to do the same. They had to go on hands and knees, the roof of the cave was so low, but it was wide enough so that they two could crawl side by side, and the Girls the same way behind them.

Dikar had to hold the torch right in front of him, and it blinded him to what was ahead, but as they went on the smell of blood grew stronger. All of a sudden, the floor ended. Dikar stopped, was bumped into by one of the Girls, heard Jimcorbin gasp: "Almighty! Look at that!"

DIKAR LOOKED, saw that the torchlight had spread out into a huge cave. But those high rock walls, that wide stone floor, were too smooth, too straight, to be the walls and floor of a cave. This was a huge room men had hollowed out in the depths of the earth, long ago.

In the wall opposite was a black hole like this one, and out of that hole came the booming of the Gulf. Like a shelf beneath the two openings was the topmost of three descending rows of huge, squared stones that end to end ran all around the cavern. They were benches where many people could sit and look at the gray statue. Thick-legged, swollen-bellied, hawk-beaked, it stood on a great stone platform in the center.

On this platform, across, the statue's talons, lay a man naked except for a narrow belt of gold around his waist, and a curiously looped, wider strap of green and gold which went down between his legs and around under him.

"Did I say there were no human sacrifices any more?" Jimcorbin muttered. "I was a liar, Dikar."

The man's eyes were closed, but his hands were pressed to his belly, and they were brown-splotched with blood. It had come from a deep and terrible gash that still was scarlet with undried blood.

The man's chest moved. He breathed, shallowly. He was still alive. Dikar thrust the torch into Jimcorbin's hand, leaped down into the cavern, bounded across its floor and up on the platform to kneel beside the man.

"Help." The faint moan came from black, shriveled lips.

"Help's here," Dikar said. "We heard you and came to you."

The bluish eyelids flickered, opened, and half-seeing eyes found Dikar's face. "True… Heard English… thought… dreaming." The lids closed again. "Water."

"Gosh," Dikar groaned. "Where'm I goin to find water in here?"

"Spring." A hand jerked sideways, as if to point. "Behind."

"I'll go look." Marilee's head was at the platform level. "I think I heard it as I climbed down; I think I know where he means."

She sped away into a growing light. Jimcorbin was running along the top tier of benches, touching his flame to other torches slanting out from the wall, held by stone brackets. They flared.

Marilee was tugging at a gold ring fastened to one of the stones in the lowest row. Bessalton came to help her and the two Girls pulled hard. The stone was sliding out. Dikar heard a tiny tinkle of water.

He turned back to the man beside whom he knelt. "She's

found it. You'll have your water." The skin, drawn tightly over a skull-like head, was beginning to shine like wax. The scrawny chest was fighting for air. If the man died before Dikar found out—"Who are you?" Dikar cried.

"Hen—Small."

"No." He had to know. "I mean are you an American? Are you one of those who escaped across the Gulf when the Asafrics came?"

"Escaped?" The corners of the tortured mouth twitched. "Yes. Escaped—Asafrics."

Dikar's heart pounded his ribs. "Where are they?" He'd found them. This Hensmall was one of them and he could tell where the others were. "Where?" He *must* tell before the man died. "Where do I go to find the others?"

"Go?" The cracked mouth was open now, in a hideous grimace. "T'Hell, m'lad." The voice that came from it was a crow's caw. "Come wi' me an' find 'em in Hell. I'm th' last—th' last of 'em all."

"Here is water."

Marilee shoved past Dikar, knelt, gently lifted Hen small's head and held a gold cup to his mouth. Dikar saw her through a gray, throbbing haze. Sunk back on his haunches, he stared at the hawk-god's monstrous thick legs and he was all empty inside, and all he could hear was that crow-caw: *"The last. I'm the last of 'em all."*

This was the end of his journey from the Mountain. The long, long road to Tomorrow had ended in the same black yesterday where it began.

CHAPTER 18

THIS FINERY IS FOR DEATH

THERE WERE murmurs around Dikar. A hand was on his shoulder, was shaking him gently. A voice, Jimcorbin's, was asking, "What's the matter, Dikar? What's struck you?"

Dikar said dully, "We're licked. He's the last—"

"The last," Hensmall's hoarse whisper repeated the word. "Last of five hundred." Marilee was supporting his head, and his eyes were open again, bright with a strange, black fire. "We licked th' Asafrics. We licked th' storms on th' Gulf."

A new strength had come to his hoarse voice, a strange flare-up. "We licked th' jungle." He wasn't looking at Marilee or at any of them. He was staring up into the fierce face of the gray statue that loomed above them. "But we couldn't lick yer copper-colored devils. They did fer us, one by one, an' sent us t'Hell tuh look for yeh."

"Lie quiet an' you'll be all right," Marilee murmured to him, but that strange hoarse babble went on.

"Yeh're white, they say, an' we were white, so they sent us tuh th' white man's Hell tuh look fer yeh an' tell yeh tuh come back tuh them, five hundred one by one an' I'm the last. Mebbe I'll find yeh. Mebbe I'll find yeh in Hell, but I'll be damned if I'll tell yeh they want yeh back, Kukulcan."

Jimcorbin grunted and his fingers dug into Dikar's shoulder. "D'yeh hear me," Hensmall shrieked, sitting all the way up now, with impossible strength. "I'm th' last an' I won't send yeh back tuh them, an' so they're licked. Licked—"

A terrible, croaking laugh broke into the words, arched the wasted body, flung it back down on the stone floor, and left it there lifeless.

"Oh," Marilee whispered.

"He's better off than we are." Jimcorbin's mouth was grim as he said that, his face lined as he bent and got fingers under Marilee's elbow, urging her up to her feet. "*His* troubles are over. Come on, let's get off this thing. Come on, Dikar—Bessalton."

BESSALTON STOPPED, half-turned toward the black hole where they'd come in. "I think the storm's ended, people." She was trying to get their thoughts off what they'd just heard and seen. "I don't hear the wind any more."

"Yeah. It didn't last as long as the first part of the hurricane." Jimcorbin was looking at the other hole, the one out of which the boom of the wide water came to fill the cavern. "But the waves will stay high for a long while yet, thank God."

Marilee twisted to him. "Why do you say that, Jimcorbin? Why are you glad that the waves will stay high a long time?"

"Because—" he checked, and his face was cut by deep lines, old-looking. "All right," he decided. "There's no sense my holding back. As long as the sea stays high, that entrance is inaccessible, and since the other one is blocked, we're safe here."

"Safe? What do you mean?"

"The Mayas of course. They—"

"But you said the Mayas vanished long ago."

"I said that their civilization did. The people themselves didn't. Degenerate, reverted to savagery, they still prowl this jungle. I knew that. What I didn't know was that their religion still lived, their religion of human sacrifice. Their worship of Kukulcan."

"That's what Hensmall called that dreadful statue."

"Exactly. That gave me the clue to the rest of his delirium. Kukulcan was their—well their human personification of their god, something like our Christ is to us.

"Sometime in the past, the legend goes, he lived among men and those were the Mayas' golden days. A long, long time ago, he went away, and their troubles began. But they believe he will come back to earth some day, and raise them again to their ancient glory."

"They made statutes of him." Marilee was big-eyed. "An' they killed people in front of the statues so that they'd go look for Kukulcan an' tell him to come back."

"Yes. It didn't work, though, and finally they gave up. But to understand this, you've got to know that in the ancient legend Kukulcan wasn't copper-colored, but white.

"So when the white refugees showed up here in their jungle, the Mayas must have gotten the idea that what had been wrong all the time was they'd been sending copper-colored souls as messengers to him, while he naturally would be in some white part of the Other World.

"The rest is plain enough. They captured the Americans whenever they got a chance, and—"

"Brought them here," Bessalton whispered. "Killed 'em, one by one. What beasts!"

"DON'T." MARILEE put her hand on Bessalton's arm. "Don't call 'em that, because we've been doin' almost the same thing. We've been killin' humans to make things better for ourselves. Isn't that almost the same thing?"

"Oh," Bessalton cried, "how can you say that? We're in a war—"

"Hold it. Hold it, you two," Jimcorbin tried to grin, but his lips were too stiff. "Right now what we ought to be thinking about is getting out of here before the sea goes down and those birds come back."

"What makes you so sure they will come back as soon as the sea goes down?" Dikar had got interested. "After all, Jimcorbin, they think Hensmall was the last one of the whites, and so why should they hurry back?"

"Because they didn't finish. I read a lot about all this when I was a kid, and I know that this sacrifice wasn't finished."

"How? How do you know?"

"His heart— Hell, Dikar, I don't want to explain the bloody business; but take it from me, they were driven from here by the coming of the hurricane before they finished, and so they'll be back. If they find us here when they come—four more whites—well, what happens to us won't be pretty. We've got to get out of here."

"Where? Where will we go?"

"Anywhere, so it's not here."

"Out in the jungle?" Dikar kept on. "Do you think we'll be safe out there? Five hundred Americans weren't. No. No, Jimcorbin. I don't want to be hunted day after day, night after night. I say we stay here an' if your Mayas come, die fightin' 'em."

"Very fine. A very fine sentiment, my boy. There's only one thing wrong with it. Look at us." Jimcorbin spread his arms wide. "Naked as the day we were born. Empty-handed. What are we going to fight with?"

"Dikar! Jimcorbin! We *have* got things to fight 'em with." Marilee was excited. "Clothes to wear an' arms to fight with. We have loads of 'em."

"We have?" Jimcorbin stared at her. "Where?"

"In here. Behind the stone we pulled out. Come." She caught his wrist, was pulling at him. "Come. I'll show you."

THEY WENT around the end of the big stone and through the place where it had been, and the light from the torches around the wall of the big cavern followed them, threw their shadows ahead of them into a dim space that held the tinkle of running water.

Dikar came into that space, and all of a sudden there was a glory in that dimness, a glory of green and scarlet and blue and yellow, vivid and glowing.

"Gosh," he breathed. "Oh gosh."

The blues and scarlets and greens were feathers, hanging on one stone wall. Cloaks woven of feathers. Belts. Head-dresses of long feathers colored like no feathers Dikar had ever seen.

And the yellow—that was gold. Golden bowls and cups and

plates piled in niches cut into another wall, hundreds of them, and there were spears of gold, gold bows strung with cord of golden wire, knives of gold whose handles were a green, transparent stone flashing in the dim light so brightly that it hurt Dikar's eyes to look at them. And all the golden things had pictures hammered into them, beautiful pictures of men dressed in the feathery finery.

"A treasure house," Jimcorbin murmured. "A fortune in the gold the Conquistadores hunted and the Indians hid from them. A fortune—and not worth a tinker's damn to us. I'd give you the whole shooting match for a bellyful of food."

"There's food here, too," Marilee answered him. "Here."

She darted to the other end of the room, where the tinkle of water came from. "Strange-looking fruits, but they must be good to eat."

Dikar saw them piled against the wall, and he saw the spring that trickled out of the mouth of a snake carved on the wall and ran into a little bowl below. It was a queer snake, it had wings.

"I get it." Jimcorbin pointed to a couple of golden chains that hung from rings fastened to the wall between the spring and the pile of fruits. "They chain their sacrificial victim here, till they are ready and since he is to be honored to the gods, they make sure that he's well fed.

"Seeing that we're going to be honored that way, we might as well take everything that goes with it. But I make a motion that we get washed first, and get some clothes on.

"I haven't forgotten your lecture, Marilee," he chuckled, "but since it isn't going to hinder us from dying when our hosts return to make us welcome, I'm quite sure you won't scold me for wanting to meet my Maker properly dressed, and in a style to which I'm not accustomed."

"Of course, Jimcorbin. In fact"—and she laughed—"Bessalton an' I can't wait to get into those wonderful things ourselves."

They were, all of a sudden, merry as they'd ever been on the

Mountain. They knew they were going to die soon, and so it seemed easy to find pleasure in small things.

"I'M AWFUL glad I washed out the black from your hair an' beard," Marilee told Dikar. "I like havin' my blond mate back again. An' I think you look fine."

"I feel like an awful fool." The only thing Dikar liked about this business was the bow he had in his hand, a bent arc of gold sweetly balanced; and the quiver of golden-shafted, scarlet-feathered and obsidian-pointed arrows slung over his shoulder. "I'm goin' to take it off."

"Don't you dare. Turn around an' let me see how you look from the back."

Dikar turned slowly. The great cloak of brilliant feathers wasn't so bad. It was light at least, and warm, and the designs that had been woven into it—of winged snakes and snarling wildcats and so on—were interesting to look at.

It was the towering head-dress Marilee had put on his head that bothered him. Why, it was half as high again as he was, and two feet wide, it was all waving green feathers and carved wood painted in bright colors. It was a silly thing for anyone to wear.

"Don't you think he's beautiful, Bessalton?" Marilee asked, laughing.

"He's pretty swell," the other Girl answered, "but I think Jimcorbin looks better, even if you did take the best things for Dikar."

"Wait. I've got an idea." Jimcorbin turned around. "Listen kids. I've been thinking about that poor fellow up there on the altar. We can't bury him, but we could at least cover him up and say a prayer over him."

"Oh yes." The smiles died from their faces. "I know just the thing," Bessalton exclaimed. "A beautiful blanket woven out of green feathers." She disappeared behind the big stone, was back with it again. "Come on."

They climbed to the platform and the Girls covered Hensmall's stiffening body. Then they straightened, looked around expectantly.

"Go ahead, Jimcorbin," Dikar muttered. "You know what to say."

"Well... look. Let's do this thing right. You stand here, right in front of this statute, and the gals either side of you," Jimcorbin moved them to the positions he meant, "an' I—" He stiffened. "We've got visitors."

Dikar followed the direction of his suddenly narrowed eyes, to the opening they hadn't been thinking about at all, the one from the jungle. A figure dropped from it to the top of the bench underneath, a red-brown, weazened man with long, black hair, a flattened, squash-nosed face, naked except for a breech-clout around his middle.

The Maya twisted, saw them, froze. But another came through the opening and a third, and they all had long black tubes in their hands and from the tunnel behind them came a great rustling that told of many more coming.

"Caught," Jimcorbin whispered. "Caught out in the open where we haven't even a chance."

"I'll get a couple," Dikar muttered, snatching an arrow from his quiver and fitting it to the bow, "before they get us."

CHAPTER 19
RETURN OF KUKULCAN

THE FIRST Maya squealed something, in evident terror. Dikar's muscles bulged as he stretched his bow. "No!" Jimcorbin snapped. "No, Dikar. Hold that pose but don't shoot. Don't move."

There were five or six of the little brown men out there now, and they made a mark one couldn't miss. "Why?" Dikar demanded. "Why shouldn't I shoot?"

"That was a sort of queer Spanish that brute yelled, and I think— By Jehosaphat, we have got a chance—a damned good chance! Hold it. Hold it, everybody. Don't show them you're scared. Just stay the way you are. Look at that!"

The brown men had dropped to their knees, there on the stone top of the benches. They were bending forward till their heads touched the stone. No more were coming out of the black hole.

"I don't understand," Bessalton whispered. "I don't understand why they're doin' that."

Jimcorbin grunted. "It's plain enough. Here's Dikar, standing over their sacrifice, the last white they had to sacrifice to Kukulcan. He's tall, gigantic in that head-dress, and he's blond-haired, blond-bearded. White-faced. They think he's—"

"Kukulcan!" Marilee exclaimed.

"Exactly. That hurricane—it broke just as they were making the sacrifice. You see? He came on the wings of the hurricane.

"Put your bow down now, Dikar, but slowly, with dignity. And then, the way a god would, in a sort of fatherly way, sorrowful because of their sins, but forgiving, beckon to them to come nearer."

"Nearer? But—"

"Do as I say! You're Kukulcan. You're their white god who went away centuries ago and now you've come back because—" He broke off, and then his eyes brightened. "You've come back because their ancient enemies, the Toltecs, are coming from the south again, as they did long ago, to destroy them.

"The Toltecs are coming in great monsters of steel, and with thunders to demolish them, but you've come to lead your children against the monsters of the Toltecs. Do you understand?"

"I understand," Dikar murmured. "Yes, Jimcorbin." He lowered his bow slowly, and slowly he lifted his arm and beckoned his worshipping people to him.

BUT THEY did not move. They stayed there, bowed to the stone. "They didn't see me, Jimcorbin. They don't dare to look at me."

"Call them."

"I don't know their language. They won't understand me."

"Call them anyway. Call them in the doubletalk you used on the beach. I'll talk to them. I'll tell them you speak only with the tongue of the gods, the ancient, forgotten language, an' that's why you brought me along to interpret your words to them."

"All right," Dikar said and then his mouth opened and sounds came from it. They were meaningless sounds, but they were deep-chested and round and booming in that great cavern like a god's sounds should be. And the little brown men looked up and then Dikar waved them to come to him, standing straight in his feathered cloak the way a god should stand, his head-dress towering over him, making him gigantic.

Dikar called the Mayas and they came, the six who'd bowed to him came, and more and more, crawling out of the black hole from the jungle, till the altar was ringed around by a sea of the long-haired, flat-nosed, brown little men, kneeling to their god, Kukulcan.

And then Kukulcan spoke to them, his voice like thunder, and the little god, Utzlcoatl, spoke to them in their own tongue and told them why it was that Kukulcan had at last answered the messengers they had sent to him; why he had come to them and what they must do.

From: A History of the Asiatic-African World Hegemony, Zafir Uscudan, Ph.D. (Bombay) LL.D. (Singapore) F.I.H.S., etc. Third Edition vol. 3 Chap 198, ff

Most of the legend of Dikar is apocryphal, but there is nothing apocryphal about the record of the posthumous court-martial of Lieutenant General Miyamara.

Miyamara himself was dead, of course, by hara-kiri, but Viceroy Yee Hashamoto was not willing that he should thus easily escape punishment for the loss of three hundred Asafric tanks, and the defeat of Hashamoto's brilliant plan to put an end to the great uprising of his American slaves.

Here is an extract from this record, a small part of the story of an officer, Major Wan Hunan. For his part in the debacle, he died under the lash on the plaza before City Hall in New York.

"I was riding in my staff car, at the head of my battalion of tanks, along the narrow defile where the Pan-American Highway pierces the Sierra Madre, between Queseltenango, Guatamala, and Tapachulai, Chiapas, Mexico.

"It was an exceedingly hot day and, since neither our reconnaissance planes nor the outflanking scouts had reported any intimation of danger, I followed orders in permitting my men to ride with turrets open. Those who could be spared from the actual operation of their vehicles were allowed to dispose themselves in the outer portions thereof, so as to be as cool as possible.

"Quite suddenly, my driver collapsed. Lieutenant Li Togo, riding alongside him in the front seat, seized the wheel, and fell dead over it. I noted a little feathered dart in his neck, then became aware of a terrific crash behind me, as the two lead tanks collided.

"In the next instant huge boulders descended from the cliffs above, thundering into the tanks all along the line, causing damage ranging all the way from a simple destruction of the caterpillar tread to a complete overturn of the vehicle.

"These gigantic stones caused a number of casualties, but the confusion they brought about, the screams of the wounded men, the shouts of those who were merely frightened, was worse than the actual damage.

"All this time not a human being had appeared.

"My superstitious Blacks were about to break. In desperation, I shouted the order to fire anyway, into the jungle, at the top of the cliffs, anywhere. As the men began to execute this order, a horde of copper-colored savages rushed onto the highway, a human wave of appalling fury.

"Many of my Blacks died, but the others, seeing a human

enemy now, fought bravely. The brown attackers wavered, and victory was in our grasp. But in that instant a great voice bellowed unintelligible sounds through the screams and crash of the conflict, and on a rock high above the road I saw what appeared to be a gigantic bird, feathers flashing in vivid colors.

"Before my very eyes, the bird became a veritable colossus of a man, blond-haired, blond-bearded. From a bow of solid gold he sent arrow after arrow into the seething madness below, and each arrow seemed to multiply into a hundred screeching savages against whose knives my Blacks were helpless...."

There follows an account of Major Human's own escape, which if we wish to believe him, was accomplished by epic feats of strength and endurance. What interests us, however, is the way he sums up this one story of what was perhaps Dikar's greatest single exploit. Thus:

"There may be some consolation, your Excellency and most honorable members of this court-martial, in the reflection that this disaster was brought about by an inexplicable raid of savages—an accident, so to speak, that could not have been foreseen—and not by the presumptuous American slaves whose puny efforts against the might of our armies are foredoomed to failure."

May the writer, in the interests of historic accuracy, point out that the "savages" were Americans, the oldest race of Americans that still exists on the Western Continent?

ABOUT THE AUTHOR

ARTHUR LEO ZAGAT (1895-1949), like fellow writer Erle Stanley Gardner, was a lawyer who forsook his profession in favor of the uncertain life of a pulp magazine writer.

A veteran of the First World War who attended City College of New York and Bordeaux University, Zagat graduated from Fordham University Law School in 1929, with the intent of practicing law. But it was the beginning of the Great Depression, and so he turned instead to writing with his fellow lawyer, Nathaniel Schachner.

Their first collaboration, "The Tower of Evil," appeared in *Wonder Stories Quarterly*, Summer 1930. Ten others followed, all appearing in the top Science Fiction titles of the era, *Amazing Stores, Wonder Stories* and *Astounding Stories of Super-Science*. They also sold to *Weird Tales*. In 1934, Zagat struck out on his own, branching out to write for Popular Publications magazines, where he made a name for himself writing detective stories and contributing to Popular's trio of weird menace magazines, *Dime Mystery Stories, Horror Stories* and *Terror Tales*. Thus he became known as "The Horror Story Man." He was also prolific in *Detective Tales, Ace G-Man Stories* and *Strange Detective Mysteries*.

When he had more than one story in a magazine, Zagat used the pseudonym of Grendon Alzee—the last name a play on his initials. For Culture Publications' sole entry in the weird menace sub-genre, *Spicy Mystery Stories,* Zagat wrote as Morgan Lafay.

He is said to have written as Anton York, which was the name of the hero of Eando Binder's famous story about an immortal. Curiously, Arthur Leo Zagat was known to some of his colleagues as Leo, but to intimates as "Bob."

Few series emerged from his typewriter over a 20-year writing career comprising an estimated 500 published stories. His longest and most famous, Doc Turner of Morris Street, ran for nearly a decade in the back pages of *The Spider.* It was one of the most popular backup series in any similar pulp magazine. Featuring the ministrations of kindly old inner-city pharmacist Andrew "Doc" Turner, it was inspired by Zagat's period of working at his father's pharmacy while attending Fordham.

Zagat's stories starring Steven "Tiger" Carlin appeared in Street & Smith's *Detective Story Magazine* in the early 1940s. Carlin was assisted by an elderly neighborhood druggist, Richard Frost.

Zagat was also known for his fantasy serials written for *Argosy,* among them, "Drink We Deep," "Seven Out of Time" and the "Tomorrow" stories. He also appeared in *Blue Book.*

During World War II, Zagat served as Chairman of the Pulp Writers' Section of the Authors' Guild, a branch of the Authors' League of America, where his legal background proved invaluable. Zagat left to join the Office of War Information, dividing his time between his New York apartment and his desk in Washington, while continuing to turn out stories. After the war, he taught short-story writing at New York University and was heavily involved in tutoring returning soldiers in the art of fiction writing. He subsequently founded the Writers' Work Shop for Veterans.

A lifelong resident of the Bronx, Arthur Leo Zagat died of a heart attack on April 3, 1949, at the age of 53. Of himself, he once wrote: "I have had no adventures in far lands. I have worked in a drugstore. I have sold insurance from door to door. I have ridden in the subway and walked the city streets with eyes and ears open. I have read Mother Goose... I do not think of myself as an artist. I am a tradesman, a merchant of tales. It is the way I make my living, and I behave towards it as any man behaves towards his means of livelihood."

www.ingramcontent.com/pod-product-compliance
Lightning Source LLC
Chambersburg PA
CBHW061523020726
47502CB00006B/2209